Shadows of Wealth and Wit

Kathy Winslower

DEDICATION

For those who search for truth in hidden places, who face lies with courage, and who learn from unexpected friendships.

This book is for you, to show that even in tough times, you can uncover secrets, find your inner strength, and build strong connections with others.

CONTENTS

CHAPTER 01: A BILLIONAIRE'S INFERNO

Ethan Harrington sat comfortably on a plush leather chair in the corner of an opulent bar. He was surrounded by the lively chatter of his closest friends. The dimly lit room exuded an air of exclusivity, the crystal chandeliers casting a warm glow over the polished marble floor, while the scent of expensive cologne and aged whiskey wafted through the air. Soft notes of jazz music played in the background as Ethan's eyes scanned the room.

"Ethan, my man, you look like you own this place! I swear, every time we step into a bar with you, it turns into your personal kingdom," Adrian laughed as he noticed the elegant patrons of the bar stealing glances at him.

"Well, my friend, it's only natural that a place like this recognizes true royalty when they see it," Ethan said, smirking as he raised his glass. "To our success, gentlemen."

Adrian Prince was Ethan's multi-billionaire company's shareholder and partner. He had thick, dark lashes framing his eyes, holding a captivating intensity that hinted at a sharp intellect and a hint of mischief. With his tall stature and impeccable grooming, Adrian was often described as the epitome of elegance.

"Cheers to that, Ethan! But I have to say, your ego never fails to amuse me. You do know that, right?" chimed in Benson as he raised his glass. He was one of their employees as well as a close friend.

"Oh, come on now, you know I can't help it. A little ego goes a long way when you're at the top of your game," Ethan replied, his deep, velvety tones resonating with a natural magnetism that drew attention and commanded authority.

"Speaking of being at the top, have you seen that woman over there, Ethan? The one in the stunning gown? She can't seem to take her eyes off you," smirked Adrian, motioning towards a lady stealing glances at them.

They all took a sip from their expensive bubbly champagne as Ethan maintained intense eye contact with the lady. His eyes were a rich and velvety shade of brown, hinting at hidden depths and untold stories. His friends were well aware of his remarkable success and the aura of power that surrounded him. They were no strangers to Ethan's commanding presence; it was like a magnet, drawing attention and admiration wherever he went.

But it didn't necessarily mean they enjoyed the fact that he was a show-stopper. As Ethan's gaze remained fixed on the elegant lady, her eyes locked with his in a magnetic connection that had grown impossible to resist. The allure he possessed had drawn her in like a moth to a flame. After a lingering moment, Ethan made up his mind. He pushed himself up from his plush leather chair and began to make his way through the crowd.

"Look at him, always stealing the spotlight from us. It's like he was born with a silver spoon in his mouth," Benson whispered once Ethan had walked far enough. Adrian, who sat grandiosely on the plush leather chair, remained silent, sipping from his gleaming wine glass.

"I bet he's completely oblivious to the envy he elicits. It's as if he is destined to be the golden boy while the rest of us struggle to keep up," Benson continued, oblivious to the fact that Adrian was lost in his own thoughts.

The sound of Ethan's own footsteps seemed to fade away as he focused on the woman. Her presence commanded attention with the way she moved, displaying a captivating fluidity. Her gown draped over her slender frame, accentuating every curve and hinting at a seductive allure. The neckline was plunging yet tasteful, revealing a hint of her collarbones. Her lips, painted in bold red, beckoned with a promise of passion and desire. She possessed an undeniable allure in her eyes, which sparkled with intelligence and intrigue.

With a confident stride, he approached the

woman, his eyes never leaving hers. A subtle smile played on his lips as he extended his hand in introduction, his voice oozing charm.

"Good evening. I'm Ethan Harrington," he said, his tone smooth and charismatic. "May I have the pleasure of your company?"

The woman's lips curved into a flirtatious smile as she accepted his hand. "I'm Amelia," she replied, her voice carrying a hint of mystery. "The pleasure is all mine, Ethan."

Their connection felt immediate, like the spark of a flame igniting in the darkness. The conversation flowed as they discovered shared interests. Time seemed to slow as they laughed and shared intimate stories. Ethan and Amelia engaged in their intimate conversation. Their words danced with playful banter, each sentence laced with flirtatious undertones.

"Amelia, a name as beautiful as its bearer. Tell me, what brings you to this exquisite bar tonight?" he said, maintaining intense eye contact with her.

"Well, Ethan, I must admit. I've heard tales of your charm and couldn't resist the opportunity to see it first-hand. Your reputation precedes you, you know," Amelia said, giggling.

"Is that so? I hope I've lived up to your expectations thus far," Ethan replied, smirking as he adjusted his cuffs.

"Oh, more than you can imagine. You have a way with words, Ethan Harrington. It's no wonder people are attracted to you like moths to a flame," she replied, teasing him.

He leaned in closer to her and whispered in a husky voice, "Perhaps it's not my words that captivate them. What if there's something about the way our eyes met from across the room?"

Amelia's cheeks flushed, a mix of excitement and anticipation coursing through her. She leaned in, mirroring his proximity, her voice filled with a seductive allure. "Ethan, I've admired you from afar for so long. Your success, your charisma—it's intoxicating. But I must confess, I didn't expect to find myself talking to you like this at this moment." She was breathless. People were so easy to impress, thought Ethan to himself. He had learned a few tricks that could make 'anyone' want to be yours. But for him, things that didn't need much effort were mostly average. His standards were anything but average.

Sensing a mutual attraction, Ethan leaned in closer, his eyes locked with Amelia's. "May I?" he whispered right onto her lips. Her eyes lit up with excitement as she nodded.

The world around them faded into insignificance as they kissed. The sensations that coursed through Ethan and the elegant lady were indescribable. Their bodies molded together, fueled by mutual hunger. The world outside faded away, leaving them wrapped in their own universe of passion and desire. As their tongues intertwined, a symphony of emotions surged within them. Their embrace offered a tantalizing glimpse into the possibilities that lay ahead.

Ethan had a lot going on in his mind There had been several reports against the products of his company, Pharmanex. They had used every single method to manipulate the media. But they still wanted to investigate the cases themselves. There was a good deal of issues left to solve for the handsome young billionaire. Ethan's dark past hadn't done him any favors either, and it only added fuel to the fire. But for now, he allowed himself to revel in the intoxicating allure of the woman by his side. He was eager to explore the uncharted territory of their burgeoning relationship.

As Ethan and Amelia continued to dwell in the depths of desire, Adrian approached the couple, as he fumbled with his phone. There was a sense of urgency etched on his face. He glanced apologetically at Ethan, his eyes tinged with concern. Amelia looked on, a mixture of understanding and disappointment flickering in her eyes. She took a step back, giving

Ethan the space to handle the urgent matter at hand.

"Ethan, it's the office. We received an emergency call. They need us immediately," Adrian said, eyeing Amelia.

Ethan, breathless, wiped the moisture from his lips using the back of his hand. His brows furrowed in frustration, torn between the intensity of the moment and the responsibilities that awaited him. He tore his gaze away from the elegant lady and focused on Adrian. "You'll have to excuse me. It was a real pleasure to know you." He smiled and with that, he took Adrian's arm and walked back to their table.

"What happened?" Ethan grunted.

"It's about a warning notice from the government that an investigation will be held," Adrian informed him. His mind raced, thoughts of the pressing issues at the office. Ethan and Adrian made their way through the bustling bar, their minds preoccupied with the weight of impending responsibilities.

As they stepped out into the cool night air, the urgency of the situation heightened their senses. In the privacy of the car, Ethan couldn't help but steal glances at his phone, cursing the interruption. His thoughts alternated between the elegant lady and the pressing matter at hand. It was a whirlwind of emotions threatening to overwhelm him.

***

Arriving at the office, Ethan and Adrian were welcomed with a flurry of activity. The gravity of the situation became clear as they were informed of the warning notice received from government officials. The warning notice looked something like this:

Subject: Official Investigation and Appointment of Sales Agent

Dear Mr. Ethan Harrington,

We hope this letter finds you well. We regret to inform you that the government has initiated an investigation at Pharmanex

Solutions. This investigation is due to recent allegations about the safety of products. As a result, we hereby declare the commencement of an official investigation. This investigation will examine the production processes and quality control measures, as well as all operations at Pharmanex Solutions. It aims to assess the adherence to regulatory standards.

To assist with the investigation, we have appointed a sales agent from the government. This agent will visit your facility to examine various aspects of your business. Their primary goal will be to assess the flow of your business and inspect production. They will review documentation and test your compliance with applicable regulations. The sales agent will have full access to your premises, personnel, and records. They will conduct interviews and scrutinize production protocols. They may also gather relevant information to assess quality assurance practices. Their findings will be documented and reported back to the government.

It is crucial that Pharmanex Solutions cooperates fully with the appointed sales agent throughout. Any attempts to hinder or obstruct their investigation are a serious offense and may result in legal consequences. Furthermore, we advise you to conduct an internal review of your processes, including quality control *measures and production protocols.*

Please note that the investigation will be conducted in a fair and impartial manner, with the goal of safeguarding and maintaining the integrity of the pharmaceutical industry. Our aim is to ensure that Pharmanex Solutions meets the required standards. We understand that this situation may present challenges for your organization, but we believe that through cooperation, we can uphold the highest standards.

After receiving the warning letter declaring the initiation of an official investigation, Ethan and his employees reacted with a mixture of concern. He immediately convened an emergency meeting with his key executives and legal team. The atmosphere in the room was tense, everyone understanding the potential consequences it could have on their business reputation. Yet, Ethan couldn't help but feel frustrated by the recurring incidents. Despite their efforts, their reputation was still being questioned.

He called for an emergency meeting with his executives to address the situation. The tension in the room was palpable as Ethan's frustration became clear.

"I can't comprehend how we keep finding ourselves in these predicaments! Our commitment to quality should be second nature to everyone in this organization. Yet, here we are, dealing with yet another incident that threatens to tarnish our hard-earned reputation," Ethan said, his voice laced with anger.

Pharmanex Solutions had employed various strategies to safeguard its image, recognizing the potential impact of negative publicity. They engaged in proactive communication, providing timely updates to stakeholders and the media. Yet, small incidents seemed to overshadow their efforts.

"We've conducted investigations and implemented measures, Ethan. But the scale of our operations and the human element make it challenging to eliminate all potential risks," one of the executives nervously explained, aware of Ethan's temper.

"Challenging or not, we cannot afford to be

complacent! Our reputation is on the line. We have a duty to our customers, stakeholders, and ourselves. We must continue to uphold the highest standards. Laziness and carelessness have no place in this company!" Ethan shouted, slamming the warning letter onto the glass table.

"We've implemented stricter protocols and increased training programs, Ethan. But we must also consider external factors beyond our control that may contribute to these incidents," chimed in another employee.

"I understand that, but we cannot rely solely on external factors. We must take full ownership of our operations. It starts from the top, and we must set an example for our employees," Ethan interrupted him mid-sentence.

"Indeed, it does," added Adrian, who had been silent for too long. "Let's be proactive and transparent in addressing this issue. We will conduct a thorough review of our operations and identify areas for improvement. I want immediate action. Our commitment to excellence should be unwavering." Everyone in the room stared at him, including Ethan. Adrian knew he was in trouble by the way Ethan eyed him.

Despite the tense atmosphere and Ethan's mounting concerns, Adrian appeared unfazed by the situation. This nonchalant demeanor puzzled Ethan, leading him to have a conversation with Adrian about his carefree attitude.

Once the meeting ended, Ethan pulled Adrian aside, his brow furrowed with a mix of confusion and frustration.

"Adrian, I can't help but notice your lack of worry about the recent incidents. There is a potential impact on our reputation. Care to shed some light on why you seem so calm?" he asked Adrian, frustration beaming in his eyes.

"Ethan, my friend, there's no need to panic yet.

We've faced challenges before, and we've always managed to come out on top. I have confidence in our ability to weather this storm as well," Adrian shrugged off his question nonchalantly.

"Confidence is one thing, Adrian, but this isn't a time to be dismissive or overconfident. Our reputation is at stake, and we need to take every incident seriously. We can't afford to be careless or underestimate the consequences," Ethan replied, anger coursing through his veins. There was exhaustion and frustration in his mind.

"Ethan, I understand the gravity of the situation. I may not wear my worries on my sleeve like you do, but rest assured, I am concerned. It's just that I choose to channel that concern into focused action rather than letting it consume me," Adrian replied, suddenly defensive.

"I appreciate your perspective, Adrian, but it's crucial that we address these issues. We can't afford any lapses or carelessness from anyone within our organization. Each of us needs to be accountable and work towards resolving these challenges," Ethan said, slightly appeased.

"You're right, Ethan. Accountability is essential, and we all need to step up our game. I assure you, my carefree demeanor doesn't mean I'm neglecting my responsibilities. I'm committed to the success and integrity of Pharmanex Solutions," Adrian assured him.

"I understand, Adrian. We're in a critical phase, and I need to ensure we're all on the same page. I value your expertise and dedication. I want us to navigate through this together, even by addressing any shortcomings we may find along the way," Ethan said, finally softening.

"You have my word, Ethan. I'll be more mindful of how my demeanor might come across. Let's focus on the task at hand and work towards regaining trust. I'm dedicated to that cause," Adrian said finally.

The unfolding situation with its potential

repercussions weighed heavily on Ethan's shoulders. As the owner and face of Pharmanex Solutions, he felt a deep sense of responsibility. Ethan experienced a tumultuous mix of emotions as he navigated his way out of his office. As he wrestled with these conflicting emotions, he remained resolute in his determination. He aimed to steer the company through this crisis. His commitment to excellence, combined with his care for the well-being of his employees, drove him to pursue solutions.

As he drove back home from his office, a whirlwind of thoughts swirled in his head. The knowledge that an agent was coming to assess their business operations intrigued him. Questions swirled in his mind: What would the agent be like? What kind of expertise and experience would they bring to the table? How thorough would their evaluation be? These inquiries fueled his curiosity.

He wondered about the criteria the sales agent would use to evaluate their operations. Would they focus on regulatory compliance? Or would they delve deeper into their manufacturing processes? Ethan's curiosity drove him to ensure that every aspect of their operations was optimized.

***

As the days drew closer to the agent's arrival, Ethan anticipated what they would bring. Before the prying eyes of government agents arrived to check their every move, Ethan and his team embarked on a journey to visit their manufacturing sites. Led by his trusted associates through the labyrinthine corridors, he carefully inspected each stage of production. Ethan was picky, for he believed that greatness was achieved through unwavering standards. He understood that the smallest flaw could undermine the integrity of their creations. Thus, he held his team to the highest degree of excellence. This commitment to perfection often left casualties in its wake. He was unafraid to sever ties with individuals he thought were incapable of meeting his expectations.

The team ventured into the heart of their most

advanced manufacturing facility. Ethan's discerning gaze scanned the bustling production floor. He watched with intensity as workers scurried around, assembling intricate pieces.

Among the sea of focused faces, Ethan's eyes fell upon a young woman. She was sitting around, shouting at other laborers to do the work for her as she sat using her phone. Sensing a hint of doubt in her capabilities, Ethan approached her with measured steps. His presence commanded the attention of the entire assembly line.

"What's your name?" Ethan's voice reverberated with authority.

She stood straight and answered, "Cindy."

"Tell me, what do you believe sets our creations apart from the rest?" Ethan questioned her.

Cindy hesitated for a moment. Her eyes darted between her colleagues and the scrutinizing gaze of

Ethan. Summoning her courage, she replied, "Well, Mr. Harrington, our products are not just about functionality. They embody elegance and the promise of a better future. They have the power to reshape industries and improve the lives of people around the world."

Ethan nodded, acknowledging her response. "You have the right idea, Cindy. But it takes more than words to bring our vision to life. To achieve that, we must strive for nothing short of perfection."

With those words, Ethan's gaze lingered on Cindy for a moment, studying her reaction. His eyes narrowed as he assessed her commitment to their cause. He recognized the potential within her. He continued, "I expect greatness from every member of this team. Mediocrity is not an option, as it dilutes the essence of our creations. But, I also believe in the power of growth and improvement. Show me that you are willing to put in the effort. I assure you, together we will achieve extraordinary things."

The team continued their tour of the manufacturing sites. Ethan's relentless pursuit of perfection in his team fueled their collective spirit. The hum of machinery harmonized with the palpable anticipation that filled the air.

***

CHAPTER 02: THE VEILED INVESTIGATOR

The sun dipped below the horizon, casting a warm golden glow across the city. A figure emerged from the shadows, stepping into the realm of Ethan's empire. Isabella Knight, a seasoned sales agent with an air of enigma.

The moment she arrived, she exuded an aura that commanded attention. Her entrance seemed to materialize out of thin air, as if she possessed an uncanny ability to navigate unseen paths. Her beauty was undeniable. Her features were sculpted with delicate precision, hinting at allure. Her almond-shaped eyes, shimmering like molten chocolate, held a captivating depth—a depth that seemed to draw others into their mysterious embrace. Her cheekbones, well-defined, added a touch of reality to her countenance. Arched brows framed her eyes with a graceful sweep. Her midnight-black tresses cascaded down her shoulders in soft, lustrous waves. Isabella's presence evoked curiosity and intrigue, as whispers floated through the air.

Employees exchanged speculative glances as they tried to uncover the truth behind Isabella's mysterious persona. Some whispered of her striking resemblance to a figure from a distant era, a muse of allure and mystery.

Isabella Knight strode into the grand hallway of the headquarter building of Pharmanex Solutions. A surge of anticipation mixed with a tinge of uncertainty washed over her. Her steps were deliberate, her movements calculated, as if she were navigating a maze of hidden agendas and concealed motives. She couldn't help but wonder what secrets lay within the walls of this organization. What motives drove Ethan and his team? Was it the pursuit of advancement, or did darker forces lurk beneath the surface?

She stood at the threshold of Ethan's office, her black eyes taking in the meticulously arranged space. As she stepped inside, her presence filled the room—a quiet confidence that commanded attention.

Ethan, immersed in his work, looked up from his desk, caught off guard by her sudden appearance. His gaze met Isabella's unwavering one. He had heard whispers of her intelligence and professionalism, but witnessing them firsthand sparked a flicker of intimidation within him. He recognized in her a formidable opponent, someone whose intellect matched his own.

"Isabella Knight," Ethan spoke, his voice laced with a mix of curiosity and caution. "I've heard many good things about your sparkling reputation. Welcome to my world of innovation."

Isabella's lips curled into a slight smile as she took a step forward, her posture conveying both respect and self-assuredness.

"Thank you, Mr. Harrington. I am honored to be here and to have the opportunity to work alongside a visionary like yourself."

Ethan gestured to a chair opposite his desk, inviting Isabella to take a seat. As she settled into the chair, the room seemed to hold its breath, bracing for the inevitable clash of minds. Isabella's smile was polite but guarded, as if she had already formed an opinion about the man before her.

"The reputation of your organization precedes you as well," she said as Ethan's brow furrowed at the hint of skepticism in her voice. He was accustomed to being revered for his achievements. Isabella's lack of reverence pricked at his ego.

"I trust you understand the importance of our work here," Ethan said, his tone holding a touch of defensiveness. "We are at the forefront of advancement, pushing the boundaries of what's possible. Our standards are very high."

Isabella leaned forward, her gaze steady. "Mr. Harrington, I am well aware of your pursuit of excellence. Yet, I must admit that there have been ongoing crises that question these standards."

Ethan's eyes widened in surprise, a mix of

indignation and realization. The fact that she had formed a negative impression of him ignited a spark of defensiveness.

"I assure you, Isabella, my dedication to innovation is unwavering," Ethan responded, his voice edged with an attempt to salvage his reputation. "Yes, I demand excellence, but only because I know that greatness requires commitment."

Isabella's gaze remained unwavering, her response measured. "Mr. Harrington, I believe that actions speak louder than words. It remains to be seen whether your pursuit of greatness aligns with the genuine betterment of society or simply serves to stroke your ego."

Ethan's jaw tightened as he absorbed Isabella's words. It was a blow to his cultivated self-image, and he couldn't deny the sting of truth in her assessment.

Deep down, he recognized that his ambitions had sometimes overshadowed the bigger picture.

"Let's both remember our aims and do our best. You can start your investigation; I have nothing to hide," he said, resigning himself to her smart remarks. He had never felt more overpowered, yet somehow he found it intimidating. He was ambitious to prove her wrong.

***

Isabella settled into her role as an agent and investigator within Ethan's company. She approached her tasks with meticulous precision and a keen eye for detail. Recognizing the significance of her mission, she kept observing and analyzing. She was determined to uncover any hidden secrets or potential irregularities. Her first step was to immerse herself in the company's operations, to familiarize herself with the inner workings of the organization.

Isabella's presence within the company grew more pronounced, as Ethan's annoyance simmered beneath the surface. He resented her probing inquiries, her nosy involvement in matters he believed should be his business. It seemed as though she made it her mission to insert herself into every meeting, challenging his authority and peppering him with intellectual questions.

In the boardroom meeting, Ethan stood at the front, presenting his latest project. The room contained all executives and key stakeholders. He had prepared for this moment, his excitement palpable as he conveyed his vision for the future.

But, Isabella, true to form, had positioned herself in the room. Ethan couldn't help but notice her presence, a thorn in his side that refused to be ignored. As Ethan outlined the project's objectives, Isabella's hand shot up, interrupting his flow. Her voice, calm and composed, cut through the room like a knife.

"Mr. Harrington, may I interject for a moment?" Isabella asked, her gaze steady as she awaited his response. Ethan's jaw tightened, but he nodded, granting her permission to speak. Deep down, he knew that dismissing her would only fuel her persistence.

Isabella's question, as expected, was insightful and thought-provoking. Her intellect shone through with each chosen word.

She probed the project's potential vulnerabilities, exposing blind spots that Ethan and his team had overlooked.

Beside Ethan, Adrian fidgeted with frustration. He had witnessed Isabella's persistent intrusions in previous meetings and was growing impatient with her interference.

"Isabella," Adrian interjected, his voice tinged with a mixture of exasperation and impatience. "We appreciate your intellectual curiosity. It's important to remember that this is Ethan's presentation. Let him present his work without constant interruptions."

Isabella's gaze flickered towards Adrian, her expression cool and composed. "I apologize if I have overstepped, but it's crucial to examine all aspects of a project. My questions only aim to ensure its robustness and success."

Ethan, though composed, felt mounting frustration building within him. He couldn't deny Isabella's intellect or her valuable insights, but her constant need to challenge him was wearing his patience down.

"Isabella, your input is noted," Ethan said, his voice carrying a hint of impatience. "But I assure you, my team and I have considered the aspects you raise. We are well-equipped to navigate any challenges that may arise."

The tensio" in the room was palpable, a silent battle of wills playing out before the gathered audience. Isabella, however, remained undeterred by Ethan's dismissive tone. She maintained her composed demeanor, unfazed by his growing annoyance.

***

Ethan and his partner, Adrian, found

themselves in a private meeting room, their expressions etched with concern. Isabella Knight's constant presence had become a growing source of worry for both of them. Ethan, his brow furrowed, voiced his frustration.

"Adrian, I can't shake the feeling that Isabella's involvement is becoming intrusive. Her constant challenges are starting to disrupt the flow of our work. It's as if she's trying to undermine our authority."

Adrian nodded in agreement, his eyes reflecting a mix of concern and frustration. "I understand, Ethan. It's becoming difficult to make decisions and move forward with our projects. She inserts herself into every discussion, as if she's trying to create obstacles for us."

Ethan sighed, running a hand through his hair. "I can't deny that she brings valuable insights and questions. But her approach is starting to feel more like an interrogation than a collaborative effort. It's becoming a battle of egos, and I worry about the impact it will have on our team's morale and productivity."

Adrian leaned forward, his voice filled with a sense of urgency. "We need to find a way to address this situation before it escalates further. Our team is relying on our leadership. Isabella's constant interruptions are sowing seeds of doubt and confusion among our employees."

As Ethan and Adrian engaged in a discussion, their conversation was interrupted by the arrival of Jane, one of their trusted employees. Her expression held a mix of concern as she entered the meeting room.

"Apologies for the interruption, Ethan, Adrian," Jane said, her voice breathless. "But I wanted to bring something to your attention. Isabella approached me, expressing her desire to visit one of our manufacturing sites."

Ethan and Adrian exchanged a glance, their eyebrows furrowing in shared concern. The timing of Isabella's request raised suspicions and heightened their wariness.

"What did she say exactly, Jane?" Ethan inquired, his tone laced with caution. Jane took a moment to compose herself before responding.

"She mentioned that she wanted to gain an understanding of our production processes. She wants to witness how our innovations come to life. She seemed quite insistent about it."

Adrian leaned forward, his voice betraying a sense of wariness. "Did she provide any explanation about why she wanted this visit? Is there a specific aim she mentioned?"

Jane shook her head, her expression puzzled. "No, she didn't mention any specific objectives. It seemed more like a general interest in our manufacturing operations. But it struck me as odd, considering her role as a monitor."

Ethan rubbed his chin, lost in thought,

contemplating the situation. "We need to approach this with caution. Isabella's sudden interest in our manufacturing sites raises concerns about her true intentions. We can't rule out the fact that she is a government official with all-access permissions to our premises and documentation."

Adrian nodded in agreement. "Agreed, Ethan. Let's gather more information before deciding. Reach out to the relevant team leads. We should ensure that proper protocols and security measures are in place. We must focus on the protection of our intellectual property."

Jane acknowledged their instructions, her expression reflecting a mix of concern and determination. "Understood. I'll coordinate with the team leads and ensure that we have a comprehensive plan." As Jane departed, Ethan and Adrian returned to their discussion. Their focus was now split between addressing the challenges posed by Isabella and formulating a strategic plan. It was a pivotal moment that demanded their utmost attention. They sought to maintain the delicate balance between transparency and protection.

***

Isabella listened to Jane's proposal about the site visit, her mind whirling with thoughts and observations. From her perspective, it was clear that she needed to delve deeper into the inner workings of the company beyond the confines of their office walls. While she understood Ethan's concerns and the need for security, she believed that visiting their manufacturing sites would provide invaluable insights. The manufacturing sites held secrets that reports and meetings alone couldn't reveal.

The skepticism and caution she encountered only served to heighten her curiosity. Why were Ethan and Adrian so concerned about her desire to visit the manufacturing sites? What secrets were they trying to protect? Diving into the heart of their operations, she could uncover hidden motives. They were protective of their work, and Isabella respected that. But she also knew that her role demanded a different perspective—a willingness to challenge the status quo and dig deeper. As she immersed herself further into her investigation, she understood that her quest would take dangerous turns.

The manufacturing sites represented a crucial piece of the puzzle—a key to unlocking the mysteries that surrounded Ethan's organization. With a renewed sense of purpose, Isabella focused on the task at hand. She would use the visit to the sites as an opportunity to gather valuable insights. Her role as an investigator demanded her curiosity, persistence, and above all, her willingness to explore uncharted territories.

The day arrived for Isabella's long-awaited visit to the company's manufacturing sites. Ethan and Adrian had reluctantly agreed to grant her request. Yet, with a lingering sense of caution, they decided it would be prudent to assign a small group to accompany her. They sent some trusted employees and a security guard to ensure her safety and prevent any breaches of security. As the tour commenced, Isabella maintained a professional demeanor, engaging with the employees who guided her through the various sections. She absorbed the sights and sounds, taking mental notes of the processes.

However, her insatiable curiosity soon got the better of her. Driven by instinct, Isabella wandered away from the main group. She knew that within the layout of the manufacturing sites, secrets could be lurking.

Isabella ventured deeper into the maze of corridors, her senses heightened. There was a subtle tension that filled the air. Her eyes scanned the surroundings, searching for any signs. And then, Isabella stumbled upon it—a door left ajar, leading to a dimly lit passage. With a mix of trepidation, she pushed it open, revealing a hidden laboratory within the company's premises. Her heart pounded in her chest as she beheld a scene she had never anticipated.

The laboratory was a clandestine space, containing advanced equipment, monitors, and scientific apparatus. But what chilled her to the core was the realization that illegal experiments had taken place within these walls. The air was heavy with an ominous aura, a grim reminder of the darkness that lay hidden beneath the company's facade of innovation.

At that moment, Isabella's cover as a sales agent was compromised. She sensed that the employees of this company had begun to unravel her true identity. The wheels of suspicion turned in their minds. Isabella could feel the increasing scrutiny in their gaze. It was a race against time—a complex dance of deception and survival.

With the weight of the discovery pressing upon her, Isabella made a swift decision. She needed evidence, proof of the illegal activities occurring within the hidden laboratory. Her analytical mind raced as she sought a way to gather the necessary information without arousing further suspicion.

Meanwhile, Inspection Officer Thompson, with his keen intuition, drew closer to the truth. His suspicions grew with each passing minute as he searched for her. His footsteps echoed down the dimly lit corridor as he approached Isabella, who stood with an air of nonchalance near the entrance of the site.

"Isabella," he called out, his voice tinged with suspicion. "What brings you to this part of the facility? I've noticed you've been wandering away from the group." She turned to face him, maintaining a composed expression, despite the rapid beating of her heart. She assessed the situation and decided on her approach, aware that her cover was at stake.

"Oh, Inspector Thompson," Isabella responded, feigning surprise. "I apologize if it seemed that way. I was actually looking for the bathroom and must have taken a wrong turn. These corridors can be quite confusing."

The inspector's gaze narrowed, his suspicion not appeased. "Hmm, it seems strange that you would wander so far from the main group in search of the bathroom."

Isabella met his gaze, her eyes holding a hint of sincerity. "I assure you, Inspector, it was a simple case of getting turned around. I'm still new here, and the layout of the manufacturing site can be quite intricate. I apologize for any concern I may have caused." Inspector Thompson studied her for a moment, his mind wrestling with doubt. While her explanation seemed plausible on the surface, there was still a lingering sense of skepticism remaining in him.

"You should be more careful, Isabella," he cautioned, his tone firm. "This is a secure facility. Unauthorized access to certain areas can have serious consequences. Make sure it doesn't happen again."

Isabella nodded, grateful that the inspector hadn't pressed further. She understood the need to tread carefully and maintain her facade. "Thank you for your understanding, Inspector. I appreciate your guidance, and I assure you it won't happen again."

With a lingering gaze, the inspector turned and walked away. His footsteps faded into the distance.

Isabella let out a breath she hadn't realized she was holding. She rejoined the other group, who were unfazed by her presence. Perfect, she thought. She knew she had narrowly escaped the inspector's suspicions. She couldn't afford to let her guard down. The encounter served as a reminder that her every move was being scrutinized, her true identity balanced on a tightrope of deception.

***

Back at her house, Isabella spread out the collected evidence on her desk—a mosaic of secrets waiting to be deciphered. The room was dark, but the soft glow of a desk lamp cast an ethereal light upon the photographs scattered before her. Isabella had managed to snap photographs capturing images as evidence. She seized documents, preserving them to ensure their authenticity and accuracy. Each piece of evidence she gathered added to the weight of the truth she sought to unveil.

As she pored over the evidence, her mind raced,

connecting the dots. She wanted to unravel the twisted tapestry of the company's dark activities. Isabella examined the documents, cross-referencing dates, names, and locations, searching for patterns and connections. Her thoughts were consumed by the desperate need to bring the truth to light. She aimed to expose the horrors that had taken place within the hidden laboratory. The weight of the evidence bore witness to the suffering inflicted upon innocent individuals.

Isabella's concentration was broken by the persistent ringing of her phone. Startled, she glanced at the caller ID and recognized Ethan Harrington's name on the screen. She hesitated for a moment before answering, aware that her carefully crafted facade would be put to the test.

"Hello, Ethan," Isabella greeted him with a calm and composed tone, concealing the eagerness that surged within her. "What can I do for you?"

Ethan's voice carried a mix of curiosity and

anticipation. "Isabella, I wanted to check in with you about your visit to our manufacturing sites. I'm curious to hear your thoughts and any insights you might have gained."

Isabella leaned back in her chair, her mind recalibrating her response. This was an opportunity to gather more information, to keep Ethan at ease while continuing her quest for the truth.

"I must say, Ethan, the visit was quite enlightening," Isabella replied, her tone measured. "The level of innovation and attention to detail in your processes is commendable. I was impressed by the commitment your team has shown to excellence."

Ethan's voice brimmed with pride. "I'm glad to hear that, Isabella. We take great pride in our work. Feel free to reach out to the relevant teams and delve deeper into your analysis. We are always open to new ideas and innovative approaches."

Isabella's heart quickened with each word. She

was realizing that Ethan's encouragement was granting her more access, which meant more opportunities to uncover hidden truths. She knew that maintaining a collaborative stance would be instrumental.

"Thank you, Ethan. I appreciate your support and the trust you've placed in me," Isabella responded, her voice resonating with gratitude. As they concluded the call, her mind buzzed with a mixture of excitement and caution. She understood that the conversation with Ethan had offered her an extended lifeline—a chance to gain further access, to explore the company's inner workings, and ultimately expose the dark secrets that lay concealed.

***

CHAPTER 03: SHADOWS OF DECEIT

The moon hung high in the night sky, casting an ethereal glow over the elegant office building. This tall structure housed the heart of the company's operations. Driven by an insatiable thirst for truth, Isabella found herself deep within its corridors, her yearning to explore more areas of the manufacturing site guiding her. As her footsteps echoed in the silence, she followed her instincts. Soon, she stumbled upon a door that seemed to lead into the darker workings of Pharmanex Solutions. Its polished mahogany surface gleamed under the moonlight, almost as if it were beckoning her to uncover the secrets hidden behind it. A sense of trepidation mingled with excitement coursed through her veins.

With a steady hand, she turned the doorknob and stepped into a dimly lit room. The air crackled with anticipation as she surveyed her surroundings. Intricate symbols adorned the walls, hinting at a hidden meaning that eluded her grasp. A hushed murmur of voices drifted through the chamber, revealing the presence of others who shared this clandestine space.

Her gaze fell upon a group of individuals, their faces obscured by shadows, their demeanor exuding an aura of power and authority that hinted at their significant roles within the company's upper echelons. They spoke in low tones, their words shrouded in secrecy and intent.

Adrian, the looming figure at the center of the room, spoke with a commanding tone. His words hung in the air, dripping with calculated intent. "The time has come to set our plans in motion. The world must bear witness to our power and dominance."

A voice, laced with a mix of intrigue and caution, responded from the darkness. "But Adrian, what of the consequences? The lives that will be lost?"

Adrian's chuckle sent shivers down Isabella's spine. "The weak will always suffer for the sake of progress. We hold the reins of power, and we will shape the world according to our desires."

A woman's voice, its melodic quality belying the ruthless nature beneath, interjected. "Adrian, we must ensure that our tracks remain covered. Any leak of our plans could be catastrophic. The government is already suspicious of us."

Adrian's reply carried an air of confidence. "Fear not, my dear. Director Bennett has proven himself to be a valuable asset. He leaks misinformation to our competitors, leading them astray while we move towards our ultimate goal." Isabella's eyes widened in shock and disbelief. Director Bennett, the trusted advisor to whom Ethan had turned for guidance, had been playing a dangerous double game. The extent of his betrayal left her speechless.

A deep voice, resonant and authoritative, chimed in. "Adrian, remember our agreement. The wealth and power we gain from this operation will be shared among us." Adrian's voice dripped with smug satisfaction. "Rest assured, my esteemed colleague. Our wealth and influence will be beyond measure. Our futures will be secure, and our names etched in history."

As the conversation continued, Isabella's mind raced, trying to absorb the enormity of the revelations she had overheard. She realized that she had stumbled upon a secret society, one driven by greed and manipulation, intent on orchestrating a global health crisis for personal gain. If they aimed to cause a global crisis, it also meant they may have a backup plan where they would emerge as saviors. She knew she had to act quickly by gathering concrete evidence to expose their sinister plot. The lives of countless innocent individuals hung in the balance, and it was her duty to protect them. As Isabella observed, pieces of a sinister puzzle began to fall into place.

Silently retreating from the chamber, Isabella's determination burned brighter than ever. She would not rest until she dismantled the secret society. However, as she left, her mind wandered, her heart heavy with a mix of sympathy and concern for Ethan, the man she had once considered her target.

The revelation that his own partner, Adrian, along with many others, were plotting against Ethan, aiming to dismantle his empire and build their own, left her feeling a tinge of sadness for him. She couldn't help but recognize the complexity of Ethan's position. He had faced challenges throughout his life, battling doubts and familial discord.

Isabella had learned about the challenges he faced in gaining his father's trust. She knew that the road to success had been paved with adversity for him. But she also recognized the need to remain focused. She reminded herself that her role was to uncover the truth, irrespective of personal emotions or sympathies. The complexities of Ethan's life were mere pieces in the puzzle she aimed to solve.

Isabella's duty was to bring the clandestine actions of the secret society to light, to expose their schemes and ensure justice prevailed. While her heart harbored a hint of compassion for Ethan, her mind knew that her primary allegiance was to the truth.

In the depths of her investigation, Isabella found herself walking a tightrope, stuck between her duty as an investigator and the lingering emotions stirred by Ethan. She understood the importance of maintaining her focus, harnessing her empathy to drive her forward.

***

Ethan Harrington stood at the helm of his company, his once-confident facade beginning to crack under the weight of mounting challenges. The allegations against his empire seemed to multiply, spreading like wildfire instead of diminishing as he had hoped. Each day brought new accusations, threats, and doubts.

As Ethan surveyed the bustling office, he couldn't escape the whispers that reverberated through the halls. The once-thriving atmosphere now carried an undercurrent of uncertainty and suspicion. Employees glanced at him with hesitant eyes, questioning his ability to steer the company through the storm. Ethan's frustration simmered beneath the surface, threatening to boil over. He had poured his heart and soul into building this empire, navigating obstacles and overcoming countless setbacks. But now, it felt as though the very foundations he had laid were crumbling, slipping through his fingers like grains of sand.

He called for emergency meetings and sought legal counsel. He launched internal investigations to root out any wrongdoing within the company. Yet, with each passing day, the accusations multiplied, the media scrutiny intensified, and his resolve wavered. He sat in his office, surrounded by stacks of legal documents and reports, doubts gnawing at his conscience. Could he salvage his reputation? Could he protect the livelihoods of his employees, who depended on the success of the company? The weight of responsibility threatened to crush him.

Ethan's heart sank as the phone on his desk jolted him from his troubled thoughts. He reached for it, desperate for a glimmer of good news to ease the weight on his shoulders. Yet, the voice on the other end of the line delivered a crushing blow, deepening his sense of despair.

"Mr. Harrington, I'm afraid I have some distressing news," the voice on the other end began, its tone laced with solemnity.

Ethan braced himself, his grip on the phone tightening. "What is it?" he managed to utter, his voice betraying the unease that consumed him.

"It appears that another allegation has surfaced against the company," the voice continued. The words fell like heavy stones upon Ethan's ears. "The media has caught wind of it, and public sentiment is turning against us."

Ethan felt his heart sink further, a sense of helplessness enveloping him. Each new allegation felt like another nail in the coffin of his once-proud empire. He struggled to find the strength to respond, unable to piece together a plan to counter the accusations. The voice on the other end remained composed, offering a hint of reassurance amidst the storm. "I assure you, Mr. Harrington, we are working to address these claims. Our legal team is investigating the matter, and we are preparing a statement to provide our side of the story."

Ethan's mind raced, his determination rekindling despite the weight of the situation. He knew he had to fight back, to uncover the truth buried beneath the mounting accusations.

He couldn't let his empire crumble without putting up a formidable defense. "I want regular updates on the progress of our investigations," Ethan declared, his voice tinged with a renewed sense of determination. "We need to be proactive in addressing these allegations head-on and must remain transparent throughout the process."

The voice on the other end acknowledged his request, offering a measure of solace in the face of adversity. "Understood, Mr. Harrington. We will keep you informed every step of the way. Together, we will navigate these turbulent waters and emerge stronger."

As the call ended, Ethan gripped the phone tightly, his mind ablaze with thoughts of strategy and resilience. He knew that the road ahead would be treacherous, but he was not ready to surrender. However, in moments like these, the haunting echoes of his father's words resurfaced, reverberating through his mind like a curse.

"You are not capable enough to run this business," his father's voice echoed, laced with skepticism and disappointment. The words had been spat out during a heated argument, a painful reminder of the constant doubts Ethan had faced throughout his life.

The path ahead remained uncertain, but with determination burning within him, Ethan vowed to silence the haunting echoes of his father's doubts. He would rise above the shadows that threatened to overshadow his confidence, defying the ghosts of the past as he fought to reclaim his company's integrity and secure its future.

***

Ethan Harrington sat alone in the grandeur of his mansion. The opulent surroundings offered little solace amidst the storm that raged within. The accusations against his company loomed large in his mind, casting a shadow over his once-magnificent empire.

It was in this vulnerable moment that his phone rang, jolting him from his thoughts. He reached for the phone and answered the call. The voice on the other end belonged to one of the private investigators he had hired, tasked with providing updates on Isabella's actions. They were to report any suspicious behavior of hers to Ethan.

"Mr. Harrington, it's Mark Smith," the investigator began, his voice steady but tinged with caution. Ethan leaned forward, his attention captured. "Yes, Mark. What have you discovered? Is there anything unusual about Isabella's activities?"

Mark took a moment, gathering his thoughts before responding. "To be honest, sir, Isabella has been rather unremarkable so far. She has been diligent in her work, conducting investigations and gathering evidence, as we expected. We haven't observed any suspicious behavior yet."

Ethan's brows furrowed in confusion, unsettled by the news. He had expected Isabella to be relentless in her pursuit, leaving no stone unturned in her quest for the truth. The absence of notable findings left him grappling with a mix of relief and frustration. "Are you sure?" Ethan pressed, his voice betraying his growing unease. "I find it hard to believe that she hasn't uncovered anything incriminating yet. There must be something more, something hidden beneath the surface."

Mark sighed audibly, his sigh audible enough for Ethan to hear. "I understand your concerns, Mr. Harrington, but we have been monitoring her. She has conducted herself professionally, blending into the company's operations. Her actions appear genuine, and there's been no sign of ulterior motives."

Ethan's mind raced, thoughts clouded by a maelstrom of conflicting emotions. He had hoped that Isabella's investigations would vindicate him, and the absence of suspicious activity left him questioning his own judgment. His grip on reality seemed to be slipping, but his ego was too stubborn to easily accept that fact.

Frustration welled up within him, threatening to spill over. "I need answers, Mark. We can't afford to be complacent. We must continue monitoring her every move, dig deeper, and uncover any hidden agenda she might be concealing."

Mark's voice softened, offering a note of reassurance. "Rest assured, sir, we will remain vigilant. Our team is dedicated to uncovering the truth. We will continue to watch Isabella's actions, and if anything suspicious arises, we will not hesitate to inform you immediately." Ethan leaned back in his chair, his mind whirling with conflicting thoughts and emotions. But with each passing day, doubts and uncertainty crept deeper into his consciousness.

In the depths of his mansion, Ethan resolved to remain resilient. He had decided that the private investigators would continue their watchful eye on Isabella. As the darkness of the night enveloped him, he found himself at the crossroads of uncertainty.

***

Isabella Knight sat in her private study, surrounded by walls lined with evidence. It was like her own sanctuary of secrets, ensuring that the knowledge she had uncovered remained shielded from prying eyes. With every piece of information locked away, it was only accessible to her. As she delved deeper into her mission, Isabella had become aware of the presence of an unseen force watching her every move. She had observed subtle signs – the flicker of suspicion in the eyes of the employees of Pharmanex Solutions, hidden conversations grazing her ears. It didn't take long for her to piece together the puzzle. She soon realized that a team of investigators kept a watchful eye on her.

This realization stirred conflicting emotions within Isabella. On one hand, she felt a twinge of irritation at the intrusion into her work. It was a reminder that her every step was being monitored. But somehow, she understood the reasons behind Ethan's actions. The pressures he faced and the allegations that threatened his company's reputation would make him cautious and protective, even to the point of investigating those who delved into his affairs.

In her heart, Isabella couldn't help but empathize with Ethan's plight. She recognized the significance of his life's work – the countless hours he had poured into building his empire. It was a testament to the passion and dedication he held for his company.

***

Isabella sat across from her boss, Director

Wilson, in his spacious office.

He had been her guiding light since she first stepped into the world of investigation – a fatherly figure who had offered unwavering support and guidance when she needed it most. Their bond had grown stronger over the years, cemented by trust and mutual respect.

"Isabella, my dear, how are you holding up?" Director Wilson asked, his warm voice laced with genuine concern.

She offered a small smile, appreciative of his concern. "I'm doing alright, Director. It's been a challenging journey, but your mentorship has helped me navigate through the toughest of times."

Director Wilson nodded, his wise eyes filled with a mix of understanding and compassion. "I've always believed in your capabilities, Isabella. From the moment you joined our team, I knew you possessed an innate talent for unraveling the truth. Your dedication and resilience have only reaffirmed that belief."

Isabella's gaze turned reflective as her thoughts drifted to the painful memories that haunted her. "You know, Director, after my parents' tragic accident, I was adrift. It was as if my world had been shattered into a million pieces. But you... you were there for me, providing guidance and support when I needed it the most."

Director Wilson leaned forward, a gentle smile gracing his face. "Isabella, my dear, you have always been like a daughter to me. I could see the strength within you, even in your darkest moments. It was my duty, my privilege, to guide you and help you find your path."

Isabella's voice trembled with gratitude as she continued. "You gave me purpose when I had lost all hope. Your belief in me ignited a fire within, pushing me to prove myself and honor the memory of my parents. I trust you, Director, because you have always been there. Your guidance has wisdom and unwavering support."

Director Wilson's eyes twinkled with pride as he replied, "I am humbled by your trust, Isabella. It is a responsibility I hold dear. But remember, it is your tenacity, your dedication to seeking the truth, that has brought you to where you are today. I may have offered guidance, but it is your skill that has made you the exceptional investigator you are."

Isabella nodded, her heart swelling with gratitude. "I am grateful for every lesson, every challenge you have presented to me. You've helped shape me into the investigator I am today. I will continue to honor your teachings and uphold the values you've instilled in me." She took a deep breath, gathering the courage to share her concerns. "Director, there's something I need to discuss with you. It's about the situation I'm currently investigating involving Ethan Harrington."

Director Wilson leaned back in his chair, his expression attentive. "Go on, Isabella. What has come to light?"

Isabella hesitated for a moment, her voice tinged with a mix of empathy and worry. "I've discovered some troubling aspects within Ethan's company, Director. It seems there's a web of deceit and betrayal that he's caught up in. As I uncover more evidence, I can't help but feel a sense of empathy for him and the challenges he's facing."

Director Wilson's face remained stoic, his voice steady. "Isabella, I understand the emotions that can arise in situations like these. Yet, it is crucial that you remain focused on your investigation. We are tasked with seeking the truth, regardless of personal feelings. It's imperative that you adhere to our protocols and follow the instructions provided."

Isabella nodded, her gaze shifting downward. She understood the importance of maintaining professionalism, even when her emotions threatened to sway her judgment. "You're right, Director. My emotions shouldn't cloud my judgment or interfere with the investigation. I will continue to gather evidence and uncover the truth, adhering to the protocols we have in place."

Despite his professional reply, Isabella couldn't help but notice the sudden change in demeanor after she mentioned Ethan. However, for the time being, she brushed it off. Their eyes met, an unspoken understanding passing between them. Isabella felt a surge of determination, fueled by the bond she shared with Director Wilson. As she left his office, Isabella carried with her a renewed sense of purpose, further fortified by his love and support. She would continue to honor his teachings, following the path he had helped forge.

***

CHAPTER 04: UNEXPECTED ALLIANCES

Detective Isabella Knight stood in the dimly lit alleyway. The faint glow of a nearby streetlight cast eerie shadows on the walls behind her. She had received a cryptic message earlier that evening, one that hinted at a whistleblower within Pharmanex Solutions. There was someone who held crucial evidence but lived in fear for their life. As she waited, her heart pounded in anticipation and apprehension. The alliance she was about to form was risky, but the potential payoff could lead to uncovering the truth.

Isabella's mind raced with questions, wondering who this person was. She realized the importance of being careful, as this could be one of Ethan's men. Suddenly, footsteps echoed through the alley. Isabella tensed, ready to face the unknown. Emerging from the shadows, a figure approached, their face obscured by the darkness. The detective's hand instinctively hovered over her holstered gun. Still, she maintained her composure, giving the figure a chance to speak.

"Miss Knight," a voice whispered, tinged with nervousness. "I am Director Bennett. I have information that could shake the foundations of Pharmanex. But I fear for my life and those close to me." Isabella's instincts told her to be cautious. As a professional, though, she sensed sincerity in the whistleblower's voice.

She took a step forward, her eyes narrowing as she tried to make out the features hidden beneath the shadows. "Tell me everything you know," she urged, her voice firm yet reassuring.

Director Bennett hesitated for a moment before finally speaking. "There are illegal activities taking place within the company. Orchestrated by those at the highest echelons of power. I own documents and evidence that expose their wrongdoings. If they find out I've spoken to you, my life will be in grave danger." Isabella weighed her options, understanding the gravity of the situation. The alliance with Director Bennett could be the breakthrough she needed. Yet, it also put both of their lives at risk. But the detective had a fierce determination to seek justice, no matter the cost.

"We'll protect you," she vowed, her voice unwavering. "Your safety is our priority. But we need the evidence to expose those responsible and put an end to their illicit activities."

Director Bennett nodded, a glimmer of hope flickering in their eyes. "I've hidden the evidence in a secure location. I'll provide you with the necessary details, but we must act soon."

As the unlikely allies delved deeper into their conversation, they couldn't shake the feeling of being watched. Unbeknownst to them, the company's director was entangled in the investigation. Ethan had deployed their own team of agents to check potential whistleblowers. The air was thick with tension and danger, and Isabella knew that they had to tread carefully. Their alliance would be a delicate dance, one where trust and caution had to be balanced. But as they stood in that lit alleyway, they shared an unspoken understanding. The pursuit of truth and justice outweighed the risks they faced. With determination burning in her eyes, Isabella knew that the road ahead would be treacherous. The sinister forces at play would stop at nothing to protect their secrets. But she also knew that she would fight, forming alliances and braving dangers.

In the days that followed her alliance with Director Bennett, Isabella couldn't shake the conflicting emotions that swirled within her. On one hand, she knew that exposing the truth behind the company was crucial.

The unveiling of the corruption and bringing the culprits to justice was Isabella's primary mission. Yet, she couldn't ignore the gnawing feeling of guilt and worry about Ethan's well-being. Every time Isabella stepped into the office and caught a glimpse of Ethan, she couldn't help but notice the toll the stress was taking on him. His once-impeccable appearance now showcased wrinkled clothes and heavy eye bags. It was evidence of sleepless nights spent grappling with the company's challenges. Seeing him in such a state, she felt a pang of concern and compassion. Even though she knew she shouldn't allow her emotions to cloud her judgment, she knew that evidence was critical to exposing the corruption within the company.

But she couldn't ignore the genuine effort Ethan was putting into saving his life's work. The lines between right and wrong blurred, leaving her with a constant sense of unease. She found herself questioning her own intentions, wondering if she should disclose the evidence to Ethan and offer him a chance to defend himself. But she knew that doing so could jeopardize the investigation and put her own life and Director Bennett's in danger. The weight of the decision weighed on her shoulders.

As days turned into weeks, Isabella found herself drawn to Ethan's side more and more. Her initial suspicion towards him had given way to a deeper understanding. It was as if she understood the man behind the empire. She saw his determination, his commitment to his employees, and his company. It stirred a sense of admiration within her. In the quiet moments of introspection, Isabella wrestled with her emotions. She knew she couldn't afford to be swayed by personal feelings. Her duty as a detective demanded objectivity and adherence to the truth. But the more she saw Ethan's struggles, the harder it became to ignore the connection she felt towards him.

In a rare moment of vulnerability, Isabella confided to her mentor, Director Wilson. She would vent about the turmoil she was experiencing. "I feel like I'm betraying Ethan," she admitted, her voice tinged with uncertainty. "He's trying to save his company, and here I am, siding with someone aiming to destroy it."

Director Wilson placed a reassuring hand on Isabella's shoulder. "It's natural to empathize with the people we investigate. We're human, after all. But remember, our job is to seek the truth and ensure justice prevails. Sometimes, that means making difficult choices for the greater good."

Isabella nodded, appreciating the support from her colleague. Still, she couldn't shake the constant worry for Ethan's well-being. As the investigation delved deeper, she knew that time was running out. She had to make a decision that would shape the future of both the company and Ethan's life.

***

Isabella hesitated for a moment before steeling herself and stepping into Ethan's office. She knocked on the door, briefly waiting before opening it. Ethan lay on the uncomfortable couch in his office. His shirt was messy and halfway opened. His hair fell like dominoes on his face. Isabella couldn't help but admire his flawless beauty. He had some features like a model. She contemplated whether she should wake him up. Before she could reach a decision, Ethan's eyes fluttered open. He got up and rubbed his eyes with the palms of his hands, completely oblivious to her presence.

Isabella coughed to gain his attention, which worked as he looked up at her standing by the doorway. "Tough night?" she said, trying to start a light conversation. She did not intend to do anything but be in his presence this time. He nodded and fixed his shirt.

"You can come inside," he said finally, regaining his composure and ignoring her question.

As she closed the door behind her, she couldn't help but feel his unwavering gaze upon her. "Ethan," she said, breaking the tense silence that had enveloped them, "I know we haven't exactly been okay, but I was thinking... we could try to put our differences aside, even if it's for one evening?"

Ethan arched an eyebrow, skeptical of her proposal. "Oh really? And what do you have in mind, Miss Isabella Knight?"

Isabella flashed him a mischievous smile. "Dinner. A casual dinner, where we can have a conversation without wanting to strangle each other. Who knows, we might even find some common ground."

Ethan smiled faintly, though his eyes still held a

hint of hesitation. "You do have a way with words, Isabella. But I have to warn you, I'm not the most charming company these days."

Isabella's smile softened, and she replied, "That's okay. Charming isn't a necessity. Your willingness to let down your guard a little matters more. What do you say?"

He sat up straighter after the words 'let down your guard. She thought. After a moment's contemplation, Ethan relented, a hint of amusement in his tone. "Alright, Miss Knight. I suppose a dinner couldn't hurt."

Isabella's face lit up with genuine delight. "Great! And you can call me Isabella, by the way." As Isabella walked away, she couldn't help but feel a sense of accomplishment. This dinner would be the turning point. A chance to bridge the gap between them and uncover the man behind the billionaire façade. She was determined to make the most of this opportunity and see where it led.

***

The atmosphere in the upscale restaurant was tense as Isabella Knight waited for Ethan to arrive. She had taken a leap of faith by inviting him to dinner. She had hoped to bridge the divide between them, even if it was for one evening. The animosity between her and Ethan had been palpable. Isabella believed that beneath the surface, there might be more to discover.

Finally, Ethan walked in, his usual air of confidence now tinged with weariness. Their eyes met, and she offered a small smile. "You made it," she said, trying to keep the tone light.

Ethan shrugged, his voice tinged with sarcasm. "Well, I didn't have any other plans, and my calendar is pretty stuffed up with stress lately."

Isabella chuckled. "How unfortunate."

Ethan's gaze softened, and he replied, "I suppose I could use a distraction right about now." As they exchanged conversation, she saw vulnerability in Ethan's eyes. There was an underlying exhaustion that tugged at her heartstrings. It was at that moment that she knew she had made the right decision in reaching out to him.

The evening wore on, and Isabella noticed the subtle shift in Ethan's demeanor. His usual guarded facade was giving way to a more vulnerable side. She found herself drawn in by the raw honesty he displayed. "I never imagined running this company would be so... demanding," Ethan admitted, a touch of weariness evident in his voice. "It feels like I'm treading water, trying to keep everything afloat."

Isabella nodded empathetically, her eyes locked on his. "Running a business of this size is no easy feat, Ethan. I can only imagine the pressure you're under, the weight of the responsibilities you carry."

Ethan sighed, his gaze drifting to his wineglass. "Sometimes, I wish I could escape it all, you know? Take a break from this never-ending chaos."

"You deserve a break," Isabella said, her heart going out to him. "Everyone does. But I understand that for someone like you, it's not as simple as stepping away."

Ethan's eyes met hers again, and there was a glimmer of gratitude in them. "You're right. It's not that simple. There's so much at stake—the livelihoods of my employees, the reputation of the company... It all rests on my shoulders."

As Isabella listened to him open up, she felt an overwhelming desire to comfort him. To assure him that everything would be alright. She saw the vulnerability he seldom showed to the world, and it pulled at her heartstrings. With all the mix of desires, she realized she had never felt this way for anyone. In a field like hers, every type of man she encountered, she never once felt how she does now for Ethan.

"You don't have to carry this burden alone," she said. "You have people who care about you, who want to support you through these tough times."

Ethan smiled wistfully. "I used to think that people cared, but lately, I'm not so sure. It's as if everyone has an ulterior motive, and I don't know who I can trust."

Isabella's hand reached out instinctively, finding its way to rest on top of his. "I'm here, Ethan. You can trust me."

For a moment, time seemed to stand still as they held each other's gaze. In that fleeting instant, Isabella felt a connection she had never experienced before. It was more than a professional duty. It was a genuine concern for the man in front of her. The desire to protect him from the storm that threatened to engulf him.

In that intimate moment, Isabella realized that her feelings for Ethan had evolved beyond mere curiosity or duty. She cared about him. And she wanted to do whatever she could to ease his burden. She understood the depth of his emotions and the toll the responsibilities took on him.

As the night wore on, the wine loosened Ethan's inhibitions, and he spoke more than ever before. He shared his fears, his dreams, and the struggles he faced not as a businessman but as a person. Isabella was there to listen, to offer a listening ear and a comforting presence.

Amidst the intimacy of the moment, Isabella's heart wavered. She had been playing a double role, walking a tightrope between her undercover duty and her growing understanding of Ethan as a person. The truth was a weight she could no longer bear to conceal. Summoning her courage, she took a deep breath, her fingers nervously tracing the rim of her wine glass.

"Ethan," she began, her voice tinged with a mix of apprehension and sincerity, "there's something I need to tell you."

Ethan looked at her with a mixture of curiosity and warmth, his guard momentarily down as he met her gaze. "Go on, Isabella. You can share anything with me."

Swallowing the lump in her throat, Isabella's eyes locked onto his. "Ethan, I'm not actually a sales agent," she confessed, her voice steady despite the storm of emotions within her. "I'm a private detective, employed by the government to investigate your company."

For a moment, silence hung heavy in the air, the confession settling like a bombshell between them. Ethan's brows furrowed, his expression shifting from openness to confusion. "What... What are you saying, Isabella? You're not a sales agent?"

Isabella nodded, her eyes brimming with sincerity. "I was assigned to work with you to uncover certain information, to ensure that everything within Pharmanex Solutions was above board."

Ethan's features hardened, his initial warmth turning into a mix of anger and betrayal. "You lied to me?" His voice carried a sting, a sharp edge that cut through the emotional ambiance they had shared just moments before.

Isabella winced, her heart aching at the pain she had inadvertently caused. "I didn't have a choice, Ethan. My mission was confidential, and I needed to gain your trust to get close to the truth."

Ethan's frustration boiled over, his hands gripping the table's edge as he pushed himself back from it. "Trust? You talked about listening, about being there for me, and all the while you were just using me for some government agenda?"

Tears welled in Isabella's eyes, regret mingling with the weight of her duty. "Ethan, please understand. I never meant for any of this to get this far. My feelings for you are real, but I had a job to do."

Ethan's anger was palpable, his face reddening as he stood abruptly. "I can't believe this, Isabella. You've betrayed me in the worst way possible." His voice trembled with a mix of anger and hurt.

With a heavy heart, Isabella watched as he turned away, his footsteps echoing through the restaurant as he left her alone at the table, the remnants of their shared evening now shattered like glass. As the door swung shut behind him, Isabella was left with a churning mix of emotions, regret gnawing at her as she sat there, grappling with the aftermath of her confession.

***

The next morning, she decided to skip going to the office at Pharmanex Solutions as her time there was nearing its end. After she submitted the report and her investigation overview to her supervisor, Director Wilson, she realized the gravity of the situation while standing by her window.

Suddenly, Isabella's phone rang, and she saw Ethan's name flash on the screen. Her heart skipped a beat as she answered the call, her mind racing with thoughts of their recent dinner and the complicated emotions that had been stirred.

"Isabella, I hope I'm not disturbing you," Ethan's

voice came through. He sounded surprisingly calm and composed.

"No, not at all," she replied, trying to keep her voice steady.

"Good, I was wondering if you could come up to my office for a moment. There's something important I'd like to discuss with you," Ethan said.

"Sure, I'll be right there," Isabella replied. She tried to hide the nervousness that was bubbling within her.

As Isabella made her way to Ethan's office, she couldn't help but wonder what he wanted to talk about. Was it about the investigation? Or was it something else? What if he regretted sharing with her?

When she entered his office, Ethan greeted her with a warm smile. "Thank you for coming. Please, have a seat."

Isabella took a chair across from him, her heart

pounding in her chest as she waited for him to speak.

"Ethan, I wanted to talk to you about the investigation," she began, feeling a mix of nervousness and anticipation.

Ethan nodded, his expression serious. "Yes, the investigation is important, and I know we're both working towards the same goal. To bring those responsible to justice." Isabella was surprised by his more open behavior towards her.

Isabella nodded, grateful for his acknowledgment of their shared purpose. "But," Ethan continued, "I can't help but feel that there's more we can do together. You're a skilled detective, Isabella, and I admire your dedication to the truth."

Isabella's curiosity was piqued. "What do you have in mind?"

Ethan leaned forward, his eyes locking with hers. "I want to offer you an alliance—a partnership if you will. Together, we can fight against the fraud, the corruption within my company, and anyone else who seeks to harm innocent people."

Isabella was taken aback by the offer. The idea of working alongside Ethan, forming an alliance to take down the wrongdoers. It was both thrilling and intimidating.

"I understand if you need some time to think about it," Ethan said, sensing her hesitation. "But I believe that together, we can make a difference. You have the skills and determination, and I have the resources and influence. It could be a powerful partnership."

Isabella weighed the pros and cons in her mind. On one hand, working with Ethan would mean a chance to have a real impact and bring down the corrupt forces at play. But, she couldn't ignore the feelings she had developed for him. There was the potential for further complications, and it could bring their professional alliance into a chokehold.

"I appreciate the offer, Ethan," she finally said, her voice soft but resolute. "But we need to be cautious. Emotions can be a liability in our line of work."

Ethan nodded, understanding her concern. "I agree, and I promise to respect your boundaries. This alliance would be professional, focused on the investigation and nothing else."

Isabella took a deep breath, her mind racing with conflicting thoughts. She knew that the opportunity Ethan was presenting was significant. But she also knew the risks involved in this alliance.

"Alright," she said, finally giving in to the pull of the offer. "I'll think about it, but we have to be clear about our roles and responsibilities. And if at any point, it becomes too much, we'll have to reassess the situation."

Ethan smiled, relief evident in his expression. "Agreed. We'll keep it professional and focused on the investigation. Thank you, Isabella. I believe together, we can make a difference."

As Isabella left Ethan's office, she couldn't help but feel a mix of excitement and unease. The path ahead was uncertain, but she was determined to stay true to her principles and protect her heart while also seeking justice with unwavering dedication. The alliance with Ethan might be challenging, but it was a chance to make a real impact, to bring down the corrupt forces that threatened their world. And as she stepped into the future, Isabella knew that the journey ahead would be filled with unexpected twists.

Ethan Harrington paced back and forth in his office. His mind was consumed by thoughts of Isabella Knight. Ever since he first laid eyes on her, there was something about her that drew him in. Like a magnetic pull, he couldn't resist. Her intelligence, her dedication, and her unwavering pursuit of justice had both captivated and unsettled him.

It hurt his ego, in a way, that he couldn't dismiss the attraction he felt for her. He was used to being in control, but with Isabella, he found himself off-balance, his heart at odds with his head. He couldn't deny the way his pulse quickened whenever she was near. There was a warmth that spread through him whenever they exchanged glances. But what intrigued him the most about her was her ability to be both a formidable investigator and a confidante. During their dinner together, he felt a weight lifted off his shoulders as he poured his heart out. In her presence, he didn't need to put on a facade of strength; he could be vulnerable, and she wouldn't judge him for it.

He realized that teaming up with Isabella was a strategic move to expose the real culprits. It was also an opportunity to be closer to her, to know her better. But Ethan was cautious. He knew that mixing emotions with the investigation was risky. He didn't want to jeopardize the progress they were making. He had to keep his feelings in check, no matter how difficult it might be.

Yet, every time he looked at Isabella, he couldn't help but wonder what it would be like to have her by his side. The idea of forming an alliance with her brought both excitement and trepidation.

***

CHAPTER 05: EMBERS OF ATTRACTION

Ethan Harrington sat in his office, the weight of stress pressing down on him like a heavy burden. He had formed an unlikely alliance with Isabella Knight. Yet, now, as they worked together, he found himself feeling a mix of emotions that he couldn't quite comprehend.

He admired Isabella's tenacity and intelligence, her unwavering commitment to justice. She had proven herself to be a formidable investigator, and he couldn't help but be drawn to her strength. Working alongside her had opened his eyes to a different side of the justice system.

The tension between Ethan and Isabella had started to dissipate over the days as they spent time working together to unravel the frauds within Pharmanex. What had once been animosity was now evolving into something unexpected — mutual respect and understanding brewed between them. As they pored over documents and connected the dots, they found themselves engaged in playful banter. This had become their new norm.

"Ah, Isabella, I must admit, your detective skills are quite impressive," Ethan said. There was a hint of a smile as he glanced at Isabella.

She raised an eyebrow playfully. "Impressive? Coming from you, Mr. Harrington, I'll take that as the highest of compliments."

He chuckled, his gaze lingering on her face. "You know, when we first met, I never thought I'd find myself enjoying working with you."

Isabella smirked. "The feeling was mutual, believe me. But I must say, you've proven to be a surprising ally in all this."

As they shared genuine laughs, their growing attraction lingered beneath the surface — a silent acknowledgment between them. It was a turning point in their relationship. They both felt it — the shifting of emotions. Ethan admired Isabella's determination and skill, her unwavering commitment to uncovering the truth. And Isabella saw beyond the billionaire facade. She now recognized the weight of responsibility he carried.

One evening, they sat side by side in Ethan's office, reviewing a set of financial records. Isabella couldn't help but steal a glance at him. His focus was intense, his mind sharp and analytical. It was moments like these that she found herself drawn to him — his passion for his work and his determination to protect his company and its employees.

"Ethan," she began, breaking the concentration that hung in the air. "I have to say, you're a lot more involved in the day-to-day workings of the company than I expected."

He looked up, meeting her gaze. "I love what I do. This company — it's not about wealth or success. It's about making a difference. By creating something that can impact people's lives in a positive way."

Isabella felt a twinge of sympathy. She understood the weight of responsibility he carried on his shoulders. "I can see that, and I admire your dedication. But remember, you don't have to carry it all on your own. We're in this together."

Ethan smiled, a warmth in his eyes that she hadn't seen before. "I know, and I'm grateful for your support. It's nice to have someone I can trust in all this."

As the words left his lips, Isabella's heart skipped a beat. The connection between them was undeniable. She realized that the line between personal and professional had blurred more than she had ever imagined. Her growing feelings for him had become a force of their own, impossible to ignore. Yet, they both knew the dangers of letting emotions get in the way of their work. They had a case to solve, a truth to uncover. Their responsibility was to do what was right for all those affected by the corruption.

Isabella found herself in a constant state of internal conflict. On one hand, she had stumbled upon earth-shattering secrets about Ethan's company. Such secrets could potentially shatter his world. They had the power to undo everything he had worked so hard to build. Yet, she couldn't ignore the growing warmth she felt each time they came near each other. The undeniable connection seemed to intensify with each passing day. She struggled with the weight of the information she held. The line between her duty as a detective and her feelings for him blurred more and more as they worked together.

Whenever their hands brushed against each other or their bodies bumped, Isabella felt a spark. There was an electric current that sent her heart racing. She knew she should pull away and maintain a professional distance. But Ethan's willingness to linger in those moments left her feeling torn. It was as if he too felt the unspoken connection between them. It was in those fleeting moments that Isabella found herself questioning her judgment. She wondered if she was being too harsh in not sharing the full extent of her discoveries with him. After all, he had confided in her about the pressures he faced, and he had shown vulnerability that few had seen. But she knew that her duty as a detective required her to remain impartial. She had to follow the evidence wherever it led, regardless of her feelings. And the evidence she had uncovered was damning — fraud, corruption, and the involvement of people he trusted could blow up this company.

The fear of how Ethan would react if he knew the full extent of the secrets gnawed at her. She didn't want to be the one to cause him pain or add to his already mounting burdens. His warm smile, his vulnerability with her — everything flashed into her mind. Yet, she also couldn't deny that he had the right to know the truth about his own company.

***

Isabella and Ethan sat side by side in a bustling café as they pored over the company's oldest records. The atmosphere was tense as they delved deeper into the web of deceit and corruption. Ethan broke the silence, his voice tinged with concern. "Isabella, I have to tell you something." Isabella looked up from the page at him.

"I overheard Adrian on a call a while back and there was something about it."

"What did you hear?" replied Isabella, her detective instincts kicking in.

"He was speaking to someone. The conversation seemed secretive. They were discussing something they didn't want others to know about. I couldn't hear all the details, but it made me suspicious," Ethan explained, a flicker of worry in his eyes.

Isabella's curiosity was piqued. "Do you remember anything specific from the conversation?"

Ethan furrowed his brow, trying to recall the details. "I remember hearing the words 'sensitive information' and 'disposal.' It could have been innocent, but given everything we've uncovered, it raised a red flag for me."

Isabella nodded, her mind racing with possibilities. "We should keep an eye on Adrian. If he's involved in any way, we need to find out."

Ethan agreed, "I already asked the team to watch him. We can't afford to overlook any potential leads." It was not that Isabella didn't know already that Adrian was one of the leading antagonists in Ethan's story. But she didn't want to lose the trust between herself and Ethan, that which she worked so hard to gain. Perhaps, Ethan finding out on his own about Adrian, might soften the blow.

Isabella nodded, understanding the weight of his responsibility. "I can see that. Your passion for the company and its employees is evident in everything you do."

Their eyes met, and for a moment, the unspoken connection between them hung in the air. Isabella felt a surge of emotions.

"I appreciate your support, Isabella," Ethan said softly, breaking the spell. "Having you on this investigation means a lot to me."

Isabella's heart skipped a beat. Her feelings for him became clearer with each passing moment. But she knew she couldn't let her emotions get in the way of the case.

"We'll get to the bottom of this, Ethan," she said, trying to keep her voice steady. "We'll uncover the truth, no matter where it leads."

He smiled, grateful for her determination. "I believe in you, Isabella. Together, we can find out who's behind all this."

As they returned to their work, Isabella couldn't help but wonder if there was more to this alliance than the investigation. The growing bond between them was undeniable. She knew that she needed to be careful. She had to maintain the balance between her duty as a detective and her feelings for Ethan. In the face of adversity, Ethan and Isabella found solace in each other's presence. The unspoken understanding between them continued to deepen. They were united in their pursuit of the truth. They dug deeper into the company's records, and their alliance became a force to be reckoned with. One that would not only unravel the frauds behind the company but also lead them toward a deeper connection.

***

Ethan's heart pounded in his chest as he approached Adrian's office. Weeks of hesitation and internal turmoil had brought him to this moment. The moment when he finally mustered the strength to confront the man he had once considered a friend. But as he got closer, he noticed something that sent a chill down his spine. Adrian was on a call, his voice low and secretive.

Ethan's instincts kicked in, and he knew he had to

find out what Adrian was up to. He moved quietly, staying out of sight but close enough to eavesdrop. The shock and betrayal he felt were overwhelming as he heard the conversation unfold. Adrian's voice was calculated and sinister. But the words he spoke sent a wave of anger and hurt crashing over Ethan. It became clear that Adrian had been working against him from the very beginning. All the secrets, all the hidden conversations, and the careful orchestration of events. It was all part of Adrian's plan to undermine him and take control of the company.

As the conversation continued, Ethan's hands clenched into fists. His jaw tightened with fury. The person he had trusted had been deceiving him all along. Adrian had been manipulating events to serve his own selfish agenda. The realization hit him like a gut punch, leaving him feeling vulnerable and betrayed. He had confided in Adrian and shared his fears and vulnerabilities. But in reality, Adrian had been playing him like a pawn in a dangerous game. Ethan's mind raced with questions, his heart heavy with a sense of loss. How could he have been so blind? How could he have trusted someone who had been working against him this whole time? The anger within him was tempered by a deep sadness. He knew that the person he had once considered a friend had betrayed him. He had been betrayed by the last person he thought would do that to him.

At that moment, Ethan realized the extent of the deceit that had plagued his company. He understood that he had to act, to confront Adrian and put an end to his treachery once and for all.

As he turned away from the office, his mind was filled with anger and hurt. He wouldn't let Adrian destroy everything he had worked so hard to build. He would fight back, expose the truth, and protect the company and its employees from any further harm. He had been blind to the signs, swept up in the illusion of trust, and now he was paying the price.

Ethan stood in his office, his mind reeling from the shock of witnessing Adrian's betrayal. The sense of heartbreak and betrayal weighed on his shoulders. It left him feeling vulnerable and raw. Just as he was trying to process what he had learned, Jane, his employee, entered the office with a stack of reports. Her usual warm smile was replaced with concern as she noticed the turmoil etched on Ethan's face.

"Ethan, are you alright?" she asked gently, placing the reports on his desk.

He turned to face her, and the anger and hurt he felt inside bubbled to the surface. Without realizing it, he lashed out at her, his emotions getting the best of him.

"Leave me alone, Jane," he said, his voice tinged with bitterness.

Jane's eyes widened in surprise at his outburst, but she remained composed. "I know, Ethan. I can't imagine how difficult this time must be for you." Jane had assumed that he was stressed about the ongoing case issues. The authorities wanted to permanently close Pharmanex Solutions.

But Ethan's emotions were running high, and he couldn't seem to control his anger. He continued to vent his frustrations on Jane, even though he knew she had nothing to do with Adrian's betrayal.

Jane took a step back, giving him space. "I understand how you feel, but taking it out on me won't solve anything. We need to focus on the investigation and finding out the truth."

As the words left her lips, Ethan felt a pang of guilt. He knew she was right, and he shouldn't be taking his anger out on her. But the pain he felt was overwhelming, and he couldn't seem to find a way to cope with it.

"I'm sorry, Jane," he finally said, his anger beginning to subside. "I didn't mean to take it out on you. It's just... I don't know how to deal with all this."

Jane gave him a small smile, her compassion shining through. "It's okay, Ethan. I know this is a lot to process. We'll get through this together."

Ethan nodded, feeling a sense of gratitude for her understanding. He knew he needed to find a way to channel his anger and hurt, to focus on the investigation and expose the truth behind Adrian's betrayal. As he took a deep breath, he found the strength to push aside his emotions and focus on the task at hand.

****

The mansion's grand entrance echoed with each footstep as Ethan paced back and forth. There was a sense of urgency consuming him. He needed someone to confide in, to share the burden that weighed on his heart.

There was no one he could trust with the truth—no one except Isabella Knight. With a mix of trepidation and determination, he picked up his phone and dialed her number. He wanted to talk to her, to seek her counsel. But he knew it was risky, given the growing complexity of their relationship. Yet, he couldn't ignore the connection they shared, and he needed her more than ever.

After a few rings, Isabella answered the call, her voice calm and composed. "Hello, Ethan. What can I do for you?"

"It's important," he said, his voice betraying his emotions. "Can you come to my mansion? There's something I need to discuss with you."

Isabella hesitated for a moment before agreeing. "Alright, I'll be there soon." As he waited for her arrival, Ethan's mind raced with thoughts of what he was about to reveal. He trusted Isabella, but the vulnerability of the situation left him feeling apprehensive. He knew he couldn't face this alone. He hoped that Isabella's presence would provide some solace.

When she arrived, there was a brief moment of tension as they exchanged glances, the unspoken connection between them more palpable than ever. Isabella's eyes held a mix of concern and curiosity—

mirrors of the emotions that swirled inside Ethan.

Without wasting any time, he led her to a private room where they could talk. As they settled in, he took a deep breath and began to share the burden he had been carrying.

"Isabella, there's something I need to tell you," he started. His voice was steady but tinged with vulnerability. "I discovered something—something that has been haunting me. I can't keep it to myself any longer." As he revealed the truth, the weight on his shoulders began to lift. Isabella listened, offering a comforting presence that eased his unease.

With each passing moment, he found himself opening up, sharing his emotions—the fear, the hurt, and the sense of betrayal that had plagued him. It was liberating to have someone who would understand the weight he carried.

But what was surprising was that he had anticipated her to be shocked at the news he told her, but she did not seem so phased.

Isabella didn't interrupt, allowing him to pour out his heart without judgment. Her compassion and understanding only solidified the bond between them. As he finished speaking, Ethan felt a sense of relief. He looked into Isabella's eyes, feeling a renewed sense of trust in her.

"Thank you for listening," he said, his voice filled with gratitude. "I don't know what I would have done without you."

Isabella offered a reassuring smile. "You don't have to face this alone, Ethan. We're in this together, and I promise to support you in any way I can." In that moment, the unspoken connection between them grew stronger, transcending the professional boundaries that had once defined their relationship. Ethan knew that he had found someone he could rely on—a confidante, a partner, and something more.

***

Isabella Knight stood on the terrace of the grand mansion, her mind swirling with conflicting thoughts. Ethan had confided in her, revealing a truth that weighed on his heart. She felt a deep sense of responsibility towards him—a desire to support and protect him from the harsh realities he faced. As she listened to his story, she couldn't help but admire his vulnerability. She saw the man behind the billionaire persona—the fears, the doubts, and the pain that he had kept hidden from the world. At that moment, she knew that their connection had grown stronger, as she found herself drawn to him on a deeper level.

But there was something else—the secret chamber she had discovered in the manufacturing site. She had wanted to tell him about it, to reveal the sinister truth lurking within his own company. Yet, the weight of the revelation and its potential consequences held her back. She knew that telling him about the secret chamber could change everything. It could lead to more heartbreak, more pain, and put him in even greater danger. The thought of subjecting him to more turmoil tore at her heart.

Yet, she also knew that the truth needed to be revealed. The evidence she had uncovered was crucial to exposing the corruption. It was information that he had the right to know, no matter how difficult it might be for him to hear. As she contemplated her next move, she found herself torn between her duty and her growing feelings. Ethan came up behind her as she stood on the luxurious terrace overlooking the entire cityscape.

"Do you want coffee?" he asked, standing beside her and gazing out at the horizon.

"Mhm, thank you," she replied, her hair rustling in the cool breeze.

"I'll be right back," Ethan said as he left her alone with the winds again.

With a heavy heart, she made her decision. She knew she couldn't keep the secret from him any longer. The truth had to be revealed, no matter how difficult or painful it might be.

Isabella's heart raced as she received a call from her director, Mr. Wilson. The timing of the call seemed almost too coincidental. She tried to steady her voice as she answered, striving to appear composed despite the turmoil inside her.

"Director," she replied, careful not to reveal too much.

Her director's tone was guarded, and she could sense his suspicion through the phone. "Isabella, I hope you're not getting too close to the subject of the investigation. Remember, we need to remain impartial."

Isabella nodded, even though he couldn't see her. "I understand, Director. I'm doing my job, trying to uncover the truth." There was a moment of silence on the other end of the line.

Isabella's mind raced with thoughts of what her director might be thinking. She knew she had to be careful, but she also knew that the truth needed to come to light.

"Alright, but be cautious," Mr. Wilson finally said, his voice stern. "We can't afford any missteps in this investigation."

Isabella assured him that she would be careful and ended the call, her mind still in turmoil. She knew that telling Ethan about the secret chamber would change everything. She also couldn't ignore the pull of justice and the responsibility she felt to uncover the truth. The evidence she had discovered was crucial to the investigation. It was information that Ethan had the right to know, no matter how difficult it might be for him to hear.

As she walked back inside the mansion, she took a deep breath, trying to steady herself for the conversation ahead. She knew she couldn't keep the secret from him any longer, no matter the risks involved. With a mix of determination and trepidation, she approached Ethan, her heart pounding in her chest. She knew that this would be one of the most difficult moments in their alliance. Summoning her courage, she approached Ethan, her voice steady but tinged with emotion.

"Ethan, there's something I need to tell you," she began, her eyes locking with his.

***

CHAPTER 06: DARK REVELATIONS

"When I went to your manufacturing site a few months ago, I discovered something. It's well hidden away from plain sight."

Ethan's eyes widened in surprise and concern. "What did you discover?"

"It was like a secret chamber, made to facilitate illegal activities," Isabella hesitated for a moment, carefully choosing her words. "From the evidence I've gathered, it's being used for illegal experiments. It's troubling, and I felt you needed to know."

His face grew serious as he absorbed her words. "How did you discover this?"

Ethan's expression turned to one of anger and hurt, and Isabella's heart sank. She hated seeing him in pain, but she also knew that the truth needed to come to light.

"I stumbled upon it during my first visit," she replied. "And the evidence points to some unethical practices taking place in there."

Ethan's brows furrowed, his mind processing the gravity of the situation. "Why would someone do this? I can't believe I didn't know about it."

"It is well hidden. It seems like someone was going to great lengths to keep it that way," Isabella explained. "But we can get to the bottom of this together. We'll find out who's responsible."

He nodded, determination in his eyes. "We have to expose this, Isabella. We can't let this continue."

"I agree," she said. "We need to act carefully. We have to bring this to light and hold those responsible accountable."

He took a deep breath, trying to steady his emotions. "You're right, Isabella. We can't let this continue. We need to expose the truth and put an end to these illegal activities."

Isabella nodded in agreement, her determination mirroring his own. "I'll do everything in my power to support you and help uncover the truth."

As they continued to discuss the details, Ethan felt a sense of relief. At least he no longer had to face this troubling revelation alone. Having Isabella by his side made the burden feel a little lighter. He knew he could trust her to navigate the complexities of the investigation. Isabella and Ethan sat in her cozy living room, surrounded by stacks of documents and files. The weight of the investigation bore down on them. But they were united in their determination to expose the truth.

"We need to be careful," Isabella said, her voice hushed as she leaned in closer to Ethan. "If those involved in the secret chamber catch wind of our investigation, they might try to cover their tracks."

Ethan nodded, his eyes focused and alert. "I agree.

We need to proceed quietly. We can't afford any missteps."

Isabella's mind raced. She was thinking of ways they could collect evidence without raising suspicions. "I have contacts within the company who might be able to help us," she suggested. "They can keep an eye on any suspicious activity without drawing attention."

"That could be valuable," Ethan replied, appreciating Isabella's resourcefulness. "And we'll need to be careful about who we share information with. The fewer people who know about our investigation, the better."

"Agreed," Isabella said, her mind already formulating a plan. "We should establish a secure communication channel to share updates and findings."

Ethan nodded in agreement. "I'll take care of that. We need to stay one step ahead of those involved in the illegal activities."

As they discussed their strategy, Isabella felt a deep sense of closeness with Ethan. They were a team, working together to bring justice to those who had been wronged by the corruption.

"We also need to ensure our own safety," Ethan said, his voice serious. "If those involved in the secret chamber find out about our investigation, they might come after us."

Isabella's eyes met his, and she saw the determination in his gaze. "We'll be careful, Ethan. We'll take precautions to protect ourselves while we gather the evidence we need." They knew they were stepping into dangerous territory. But the trust and bond between them gave them the strength to face the challenges ahead. As they wrapped up their planning, Isabella felt a sense of relief. She knew that together, they were a formidable force. Somehow, deep in her heart, she knew that as long as Ethan was with her, everything would be fine.

"We can do this," Ethan said, a flicker of hope in

his eyes.

"We can," Isabella agreed, a sense of confidence filling her heart. "We'll uncover the truth and put an end to the corruption."

After the detailed meeting with Ethan about their next move, Isabella decided to go meet Mr. Wilson. After exposing the secret chamber to Ethan, she had felt more relieved than ever. Working like this with him not only benefited her investigation but also brought her a sense of assurance. So, she took a car to Mr. Wilson's office to tell him about their plan to take down the corrupt.

When she arrived in front of her office building, she noticed Mr. Wilson at a nearby café, talking to Director Benson from Pharmanex Solutions. Seeing him was shocking for Isabella, as she had warned him to stay out of the public eye.

Isabella's heart raced with curiosity and suspicion as she followed her director, Mr. Wilson, and Mr.

Benson. Something about their secretive meeting seemed off. She couldn't shake the feeling that there was more to this encounter than met the eye.

Staying hidden behind a newspaper at a nearby table, Isabella kept her eyes fixed on the two men. They were deep in conversation, their voices hushed, and their expressions guarded. She strained to catch snippets of their discussion, but their words remained elusive, leaving her perplexed.

As she watched them exchange glances, a sense of unease settled over her. Mr. Wilson had always been a father-like figure to her, a trusted mentor who had guided her throughout her career. Yet, this clandestine meeting raised questions in her mind about his true intentions.

When Mr. Benson slid an envelope across the table to Mr. Wilson, Isabella's intrigue intensified. Her instincts told her that whatever was inside that envelope held crucial information. She needed to find out what it was.

As the two men rose to leave, Isabella acted quickly. She slipped out of the café, maintaining a safe distance as she followed them to their next destination. The trail led them to a secluded park, where they sat on a bench, continuing their discussion. Isabella found a spot behind a tree, hidden from their view yet close enough to hear their conversation.

The air was thick with tension, and Isabella strained to hear their conversation.

"I've taken care of the evidence against Ethan's company," Mr. Benson whispered, a smug smile playing on his lips. "No one will ever suspect that I was involved."

Mr. Wilson nodded, his expression cold and calculating. "Good. We can't have any loose ends."

"What about the detective, Isabella?" Mr. Benson asked, his eyes darting around the area as if he expected her to appear at any moment. "She's been asking too many questions, and I'm afraid she might know more than we realize."

A sense of apprehension washed over Isabella as she continued to listen to her director's response. She had never imagined Mr. Wilson being involved in such deception and betrayal. "Don't worry," Mr. Wilson said, his voice low and menacing. "I'll take care of her. She won't be a problem for us anymore."

Isabella's heart pounded in her chest. She realized the depth of the conspiracy that had ensnared her own director. She had trusted him, and now she felt a profound sense of betrayal. Mr. Benson leaned in even closer, his voice a mere whisper. "Make sure it's done quietly. We can't afford any mistakes."

Mr. Wilson nodded again, a sinister glint in his eyes. "I'll handle it. She won't even see it coming."

Isabella's mind raced with a mix of fear and determination. She knew she had to act if she wanted to protect herself and expose the truth. As the two men concluded their conversation, Isabella watched them leave the park, her mind already formulating a plan. She needed to stay one step ahead of them and find a way to gather enough evidence to bring down the conspiracy.

The pieces of the puzzle were falling into place. She couldn't ignore the mounting evidence of Mr. Wilson's involvement in the conspiracy against Ethan. His peculiar behavior whenever she mentioned Ethan and his urgency to hire her for the case despite her lack of recent experience. Everything now seemed like a calculated move to keep a close eye on her and manipulate the situation.

She had looked up to Mr. Wilson as a mentor and father figure. But now she saw him in a different light—a man willing to betray and deceive for personal gain. It hurt to think that someone she had respected and admired could be so callous and deceitful. She felt a mix of anger, sorrow, and disappointment. Anger at the deception, sorrow for the loss of trust, but most of all, there was disappointment in herself for not seeing the signs sooner.

She couldn't help but question her judgment. She wondered how she had allowed herself to be deceived by someone she thought she knew so well. The realization that Mr. Wilson was willing to get rid of her, even harm her, sent chills down her spine. It was a sobering reminder of the dangers she faced in pursuing the truth. But she refused to remain silent. If anything, the betrayal fueled her determination to uncover the full extent of the corruption.

With every step forward, Isabella would carry the weight of her hurt and betrayal. She would turn it into an unwavering resolve to seek the truth. The detective would become a force to be reckoned with. Nothing would deter her from her quest for justice.

This incident had only made her decision easier, for she knew now the path ahead became clear. With the help of Ethan, she would do everything in her power to make these criminals face adversity.

***

Isabella knew she had to be cautious if she wanted to protect herself. She had to continue her investigation without arousing suspicion. Sending in her resignation seemed like the best course of action. With a heavy heart and a steely resolve, she walked into Mr. Wilson's office, her emotions masked behind a composed facade. She took a deep breath as she entered the office.

"Mr. Wilson," Isabella began, her voice steady, "I need to talk to you about the investigation." Mr. Wilson looked up from his desk, his expression guarded. "What is it, Isabella?"

"I've been thinking a lot about this case. I've come to the conclusion that the danger involved is too great," Isabella said, carefully choosing her words. "I believe it's best if I step back from the investigation."

Mr. Wilson's brows furrowed. "Step back? But we need you on this case, Isabella. You're the best we have."

Isabella nodded, maintaining her facade of uncertainty. "I understand, but I can't shake the feeling that I'm in over my head. The people we're dealing with are dangerous, and I fear for my safety."

Mr. Wilson leaned back in his chair, studying Isabella. "I understand your concerns, but we can provide you with extra security. You don't need to worry."

"I appreciate that. I need some time to think things through," Isabella said, feigning hesitation. "I believe it's in my best interest to resign from the case, at least for now."

Mr. Wilson's face softened with understanding. "Alright, Isabella. Your safety is paramount, and I won't force you to do anything you're uncomfortable with. Take the time you need."

With that, Isabella's resignation was set in motion. She had successfully planted the seed of doubt in Mr. Wilson's mind, making him believe that she was stepping back from the investigation due to fear for her safety.

As she walked out of his office, she couldn't help but feel a pang of guilt. Deceiving the man who had once been a mentor to her weighed on her conscience. But her focus now shifted to her next move—working with Ethan to gather evidence against the conspirators. Isabella knew that she needed to gain Ethan's complete trust. The knowledge of the powerful adversaries they were up against weighed heavily on her mind, making her fear for her own life and for Ethan's safety.

***

Late one evening, with a knot of anxiety in her stomach, Isabella decided it was time to share everything she had uncovered. They needed to plan and be prepared for the potential consequences of their actions. With a sense of urgency, she drove to Ethan's mansion, her heart pounding with trepidation. As she reached the grand entrance, Isabella was greeted by the imposing structure of the mansion, a stark contrast to the turmoil inside her mind.

Stepping out of her car to meet Ethan, a sense of foreboding gripped her. Before she could comprehend what was happening, a black van screeched to a halt in front of her, blocking her path.

The doors swung open, and several men dressed in all black jumped out, surrounding her like a pack of wolves. Fear washed over her, her heart pounding. She knew these men were not there for a friendly conversation.

One of them stepped forward, his cold eyes locking onto Isabella's. "Get in the van," he commanded, his voice laced with menace.

Isabella's mind raced with panic and adrenaline, and she instinctively resisted. "Who are you? What do you want?" she demanded, trying to maintain a facade of courage despite her trembling limbs. But her defiance only seemed to amuse the men.

Without warning, they closed in, grabbing her arms and attempting to force her into the van. Isabella struggled, fighting with every ounce of strength she could muster. But their grip was relentless, and she found herself overpowered and unable to break free. Panic surged through her veins as she realized the dire situation she was in. Her heart sank as she wondered if this was the end of her quest for the truth.

"Don't fight back too much, princess. We'll have some fun tonight," the man said, his face just inches from hers.

Just as Isabella thought all hope was lost, a familiar voice rang out from the front gate of the mansion. "Let her go!"

Ethan's commanding voice echoed through the air, and Isabella's heart leaped with relief. Her instincts had led her to the right person to confide in, and now, she hoped he would be her savior. The men hesitated for a moment, their attention diverted to Ethan's sudden appearance. It was the window of opportunity

Isabella needed. With a surge of adrenaline, she managed to break free from their grasp and stumbled back.

Ethan's eyes blazed with fury as he rushed towards her, a protective instinct taking over. "Stay away from her! You're surrounded by my men. And they won't hesitate to shoot," he warned the men, his voice firm and resolute.

The tension in the air was palpable, and Isabella felt the weight of the dangerous situation they were in. She could see the conflict in Ethan's eyes – the desire to protect her and the need to confront the threat head-on. Before anything else could happen, the men exchanged glances with each other. They were calculating their odds. They seemed to realize that they were outnumbered. And with one last menacing glare at Isabella, they retreated to their van and sped away.

Isabella was left trembling, her heart still pounding in her chest. She glanced at Ethan, gratitude and fear mingling in her eyes. "Thank you," she managed to say, her voice shaky.

Ethan's concern was evident as he stepped closer to her, his hand resting on her shoulder. "Are you alright?" he asked, his voice filled with genuine concern.

Isabella nodded, taking a deep breath to steady herself. "Yes, I'm fine. They were after me, not you," she replied, her mind racing with the implications of the attack.

Ethan's jaw tightened, his eyes narrowing as he absorbed her words. "Why would anyone be after you?" he asked, his protective instincts still on high alert.

Isabella hesitated, unsure of how much she should reveal. But she knew she could trust Ethan. "It's connected to the investigation. I think they know I'm getting too close to the truth," she admitted.

Ethan's expression darkened, and a steely

determination filled his eyes. "Then we'll face this together," he said. "No matter what, I won't let anything happen to you."

Isabella felt a mix of emotions – fear, relief, and a growing sense of trust in the man standing before her. She knew that their alliance had become something more, something deeper. With the threat averted, Ethan led Isabella into the safety of his grand mansion. The warm glow of chandeliers illuminated the luxurious interiors. The air carried the comforting scent of a crackling fireplace.

"Come on, let's go inside," Ethan said, guiding Isabella toward the elegant sitting room. He couldn't shake the feeling of protectiveness that surged through him. He wanted to shield her from any further harm.

The butler, James, appeared with his characteristic poise. "Mr. Harrington, may I offer you both something to eat or drink?" he inquired.

Ethan glanced at Isabella, his concern evident in

his eyes. "Yes, James, please prepare some of our finest dishes for Miss Isabella. And bring a bottle of my favorite wine," he said, his voice gentle and caring.

Isabella felt touched by his thoughtfulness, but a part of her felt uneasy. She knew she had to maintain her focus on the investigation. She couldn't let herself be swayed by Ethan's kindness.

Yet, she couldn't deny the warmth that washed over her as she saw him taking such care of her. As they settled into the plush chairs, Ethan couldn't help but let his guard down around her. He had always been the one in control, but Isabella's presence had a way of breaking through his defenses. He felt drawn to her strength, her determination.

"I'm sorry you had to go through that," Ethan said, his voice sincere. "I never imagined that anyone would go to such lengths to stop us."

Isabella nodded, her gratitude for his concern evident in her eyes. "It's a dangerous path we're treading, but we can make a difference," she said.

Ethan leaned forward, his eyes searching hers. "I believe in you, Isabella. You've shown me how fearless you can be in pursuing the truth," he said, a hint of admiration in his voice.

He placed a finger under her chin and lifted it up, "Now allow me to do what it takes for me to become fearless."

Isabella felt her cheeks flush at his words. She was feeling a flutter of emotions she couldn't ignore. But she reminded herself that she needed to remain focused on their mission.

The butler returned with a tray of delicacies and an expensive bottle of wine. Isabella couldn't help but marvel at the grandeur of the mansion. It was a stark contrast to her own humble apartment. She felt like an outsider in this world of wealth and privilege.

"Ethan…" Isabella started, keeping her voice

steady. He looked up from the food to look at her as she continued, "There is a lot you need to know."

***

CHAPTER 07: BETRAYAL'S WEB

As they were seated in the study of Ethan's sprawling mansion after the lavish dinner, the room exuded an air of elegance and sophistication. Adorned with rich wood paneling and ornate bookshelves filled with leather-bound volumes, the soft glow of an antique chandelier bathed the room in warm, golden light. It created an ambiance of comfort and luxury.

The study's walls were adorned with tasteful artwork, depicting scenes from various eras, hinting at the eclectic taste and interests of its owner. A plush Persian rug adorned the polished hardwood floor, adding a touch of opulence to the space.

Ethan looked at her, concern etched on his face. "So, what is it that you wanted to tell me, Isabella? You look upset," he said, his voice filled with concern.

"I discovered that Mr. Wilson has been using me to gain power within the company," Isabella revealed. She kept her voice steady despite the turmoil inside her. "He and others are involved in a conspiracy to take control and cut both of us out."

Ethan's eyes widened with shock and disbelief. "Mr. Benson? Him too? He was my father's most trusted companion," he said, his voice tinged with disbelief.

"I know, Ethan, but he's been deceiving both of us," Isabella said, her voice filled with frustration. "He used my investigation as a tool to further his own agenda, and I played right into his hands."

A grand fireplace stood on the opposite wall, its mantle adorned with tasteful decorations and family photographs. They were a reminder of the ties that bound Ethan to his legacy. The fire crackled, casting dancing shadows on the walls.

Ethan's jaw clenched with anger as he processed the information. "How could he betray us like this?" he muttered, a mix of emotions clouding his features. Isabella took a deep breath, steadying herself.

"He made me believe that he was on our side, but he was manipulating me all along. He threatened my safety and made it clear that he had no qualms about taking us out if we became a hindrance to his plans," she explained. Her voice trembled with suppressed emotion.

Ethan's eyes narrowed with determination. "We can't let him get away with this," he said. "We need to gather all the evidence as soon as possible and stop him before he causes any more harm."

Isabella nodded, grateful for his unwavering support. "I agree, Ethan. We have to be careful, though. Mr. Wilson is dangerous, and he has powerful allies," she warned, a note of caution in her voice. The moonlight spilled in, illuminating the room with a silvery glow. It added an air of mystery to the already somber atmosphere. The floor-to-ceiling windows offered a breathtaking view of the mansion's manicured gardens.

"I won't let him hurt you or anyone else," Ethan

vowed, his gaze locking with hers. "We'll face this together like we've faced everything else." Isabella felt a surge of gratitude for Ethan's strength and determination. Despite the dangers they faced, she knew she could trust him to stand by her side.

"I should get going, it's getting late," Isabella said after a while. She broke the comfortable silence between them. Ethan snapped back from his thoughts and sat up straighter, all alert.

"You can't go, it's too dangerous to be alone," he said.

Isabella smirked and then replied, "Ethan, I am a Professional Investigator and I am more than capable of taking care of myself." She was faintly smiling, but Ethan furrowed his eyebrows.

"Like you did back there in front of my mansion?" he said, his voice flat.

Isabella felt the blood rush to her cheeks due to

pure embarrassment. When Ethan noticed the flustered look on her face, he added, "It's okay. You can stay here for tonight," he suggested. A smile formed on his lips as he spoke. Isabella understood that going back to her house right now was a bad idea, so she didn't argue much.

Despite the weight of the situation, the room exuded an air of elegance and refinement. It was a reflection of Ethan's status as a billionaire and leader of a powerful corporation. But beneath the opulence, Isabella sensed the vulnerability that plagued its owner. It made her more determined than ever to protect the man sitting across from her.

Ethan, on the other hand, was determined to ensure she felt safe and protected, especially after the scare with the mysterious men in black. As they walked through the grand halls of his mansion, Ethan's luxurious lifestyle was evident in every gesture. He made sure she was comfortable, offering her a luxurious guest room to rest in. As the night grew late, Ethan led Isabella down a corridor adorned with elegant artwork. He stopped at a carved wooden door and turned to her with a warm smile.

"This will be your room for the night," he said, pushing the door open, revealing a spacious and beautifully decorated guest room. Isabella stepped inside, her eyes taking in the luxurious surroundings.

Ethan smiled, pleased with her reaction. "I'm glad you like it. You deserve to be pampered and feel safe here," he said, his voice gentle and caring. Isabella turned to face him, their eyes meeting, and she couldn't help but notice the genuine concern in his gaze. It touched her heart, making her feel seen and valued in a way she hadn't experienced before.

"Thank you, Ethan," she said, her voice soft and sincere. "For everything you've done tonight. I can't believe how much you've looked out for me."

Ethan's smile softened, and he stepped closer to her. "It's the least I can do," he said. "You've been a crucial ally, and I couldn't bear to see anything happen to you."

Isabella felt a flutter in her chest at his words, the warmth of his presence enveloping her. She knew they were in the midst of a dangerous investigation, but at that moment, all she could think about was the man in front of her.

As if sensing her emotions, Ethan reached out and brushed a strand of hair away from her face. "We'll get through this together, Isabella," he said, his voice unwavering. "I won't let anything happen to you."

Isabella's heart swelled with a mix of emotions. She knew they had a difficult path ahead, but she also felt reassured by his presence.

"Thank you," she said again, her voice above a whisper. "I feel safer with you than I ever have before."

Ethan's eyes held a tender gaze, and he leaned in slightly, his breath brushing against her cheek. "You should get some rest," he said. "We have a lot of work to do tomorrow."

Isabella nodded, reluctant to take her eyes away from his. "Goodnight, Ethan," she said, her voice tinged with a hint of vulnerability.

"Goodnight, Isabella," he replied, his voice filled with warmth. He lingered for a moment before stepping back with a soft smile.

Isabella settled into the plush bed. She couldn't help but feel a sense of gratitude for the man who had unexpectedly entered her life. In the silence of the guest room, Isabella closed her eyes, feeling a mix of emotions swirling inside her.

She knew that their connection was far from ordinary. It was as if he wanted to ensure her well-being and comfort, and it made her heart skip a beat. As she drifted off to sleep, she couldn't help but wonder what the future held for them. But for now, she allowed herself to savor the intimacy of the moment.

The night wore on, and the mansion settled into a quiet stillness. While Ethan found himself alone in his study, his mind consumed with thoughts of Isabella. The events of the day had been intense and emotionally charged. He couldn't shake the feelings that had been awakened within him. He had always prided himself on being a strong and self-reliant man. Yet, Isabella's presence in his life had thrown him off balance. The way she faced danger and the determination with which she pursued the truth had left a deep impression on him. She was smart, courageous, and independent – qualities that both impressed and captivated him.

But it was more than admiration that he felt for her. The more time he spent with Isabella, the more he found himself drawn to her on a deeper level. Her laughter was like a melody that warmed his heart. Her smile had the power to ease his worries even in the darkest of times. He couldn't deny the growing attraction he felt toward her, and it both exhilarated and scared him. He knew that getting involved with her on a personal level could complicate things, given the dangerous circumstances they were in. Yet, he found it hard to resist the magnetic pull between them.

***

Early morning, the next day, as Ethan sat in his study, he found himself lost in thoughts of her. Isabella's radiant smile, the way her eyes sparkled when she was determined. It was both a blessing and a curse to have found someone who understood the weight of his responsibilities and the struggles he faced.

Ethan knew that their alliance was born out of necessity, but he couldn't help but wonder if it could grow into something more. He was torn between his desire to protect her and the fear of putting her in harm's way.

With a heavy heart and a mind filled with conflicting emotions, Ethan finally acknowledged his feelings for Isabella. He knew that he had to be cautious, and he also couldn't deny the growing attraction and connection he felt toward her. Ethan vowed to protect Isabella with all his strength.

Ethan's phone buzzed, and he saw Adrian's name on the caller ID. He took a deep breath, knowing he had to maintain his composure despite the hurt and anger he felt from the betrayal he had overheard. He answered the call, his voice steady.

"Hey, Adrian, what's up?" Ethan said, trying to sound nonchalant.

"Hey, Ethan! I wanted to let you know that I'll be holding a press conference tomorrow morning. I thought it was time we address the allegations. We need to show the public that we're taking them seriously," Adrian replied.

Ethan clenched his jaw, the memory of hearing Adrian's conversation still fresh in his mind. "That's a good idea," he replied, trying to keep his tone neutral.

"At this point, it's crucial that we address the situation, to assure our stakeholders that we're working to maintain the company's reputation."

"Exactly!" Adrian said, sounding enthusiastic. "I've been working on a statement. It should show that we're committed to transparency and accountability."

Ethan fought the urge to confront Adrian about the phone call, not wanting to tip his hand too soon. Instead, he decided to play it cool and gather more information before taking any action. "That sounds great, Adrian. Let me know if you need any help with the statement," Ethan said, trying to sound supportive.

"Thanks, Ethan. I appreciate it," Adrian replied. "I'll send you a draft later, and we can go over it together."

"Sure, sounds good," Ethan said, forcing a smile. "Let's make sure we address everything and put this whole thing behind us."

As the conversation continued, Ethan kept his emotions in check. He knew he had to stay focused on their investigation and gather enough evidence before confronting Adrian about his suspicious activities.

After hanging up, Ethan took a deep breath, trying to process everything he had heard. He couldn't ignore the fact that Adrian might be involved in the conspiracy. But he also knew he had to be cautious and patient, not letting his emotions cloud his judgment. As the night stretched on, Ethan found himself bracing for the storm that lay ahead. The journey to unravel the truth had begun. He knew it was a path that could lead to both salvation and destruction.

***

The morning sun cast a warm glow over the breakfast table. Isabella and Ethan sat, contemplating the day that lay ahead. The aroma of freshly brewed coffee filled the air, but neither of them seemed to have much of an appetite. Isabella looked up from her cup, meeting Ethan's gaze. There was a determination in her eyes, a fire that mirrored the resolve in his own. They both knew what they were up against, and they were ready to face it head-on.

"Are you sure about this, Ethan?" Isabella finally broke the silence, her voice soft but unwavering.

Ethan nodded, his jaw set with determination. "Yes, we can't let them get away with this. They've taken advantage of our trust for too long."

Isabella nodded in agreement, a sense of camaraderie growing between them. "I've gathered enough evidence to expose their corruption, but we need to be careful. They won't go down without a fight," she warned.

Ethan's lips quirked into a half-smile. "Good thing we're not afraid of a fight," he replied, a glint of determination in his eyes.

As they continued to talk, their plan took shape. They decided to gather all the evidence they had separately. This was to ensure that nothing would be lost or compromised. Isabella would work from her end, pulling strings to expose the corruption within the company's upper echelons. Meanwhile, Ethan would dig deeper into the mysterious connections and power players.

Throughout the day, he tried to push aside his feelings. He had attempted to focus on their mission and the investigation at hand. But every time he looked at Isabella, he couldn't help but feel a sense of protectiveness toward her. He wanted to shield her from harm.

"We need to be prepared for anything," Isabella cautioned. Her eyes searched his for reassurance. Ethan reached across the table, gently placing his hand on hers. "I trust you, Isabella. And I know we can do this together," he said, his voice filled with conviction.

A wave of warmth washed over Isabella as she felt his touch. She couldn't help but feel a sense of gratitude for the man sitting across from her. In the midst of chaos and danger, Ethan had become more than an ally; he had become a partner she could rely on.

As they finished their breakfast, they both knew that the battle ahead would be arduous and perilous. They were up against a web of corruption and deceit that reached the highest levels of power. But they were also armed with the truth, and that was a weapon they intended to use wisely.

***

The day of the press conference arrived, and the tension in the air was palpable. The media had been buzzing with speculations about the allegations against Ethan's company. The public was hungry for answers. The appointed time drew near, and the grand hall of the hotel was abuzz with reporters and cameras, all eager to witness the unfolding drama. Ethan and Adrian stood side by side at the podium, both dressed in impeccable suits, projecting an image of calm and control. The room fell silent as the press conference began, and a hushed anticipation filled the air. Ethan stepped forward, his voice steady as he addressed the gathered crowd.

"Ladies and gentlemen, thank you for being here today. I want to address the allegations that have been circulating about our company," he began, his gaze unwavering as he looked into the cameras.

"We take these allegations seriously. I want to assure you all that we are conducting a thorough internal investigation to get to the truth. Our company's reputation is built on a foundation of trust, and we are committed to upholding those values," Ethan continued, his voice firm and resolute.

A sea of reporters and cameras faced him, eager for answers. They pressed him with questions about the specific allegations and the individuals involved. Ethan answered each query with careful precision, neither confirming nor denying anything, but always reiterating their commitment to a transparent investigation.

Beside him, Adrian interjected with confidence,

adding to Ethan's carefully crafted narrative. "We are cooperating with the authorities, and we are confident that the truth will come to light. Our company has a longstanding track record of excellence, and we stand by our products and our team," he stated, projecting an air of assurance.

Isabella observed from the sidelines, her professional façade intact even though her heart was racing. She knew the truth they were seeking was far from the polished surface of the press conference. She remained discreet and alert, her mind focused on the bigger picture.

As the press conference continued, Ethan maintained his composure, but inside, he wrestled with conflicting emotions. He couldn't shake the feeling that there was something more beneath the surface, something he needed to uncover at all costs.

The memory of hearing Adrian's suspicious phone call still gnawed at him. He kept his guard up, not wanting to reveal his suspicions too soon.

Finally, after what felt like an eternity, the press conference concluded. Reporters dispersed, and the room emptied. Isabella approached Ethan, her expression unreadable.

"You did well back there," she commented, her voice soft and professional.

Ethan offered her a small smile, but his mind was still preoccupied with lingering doubts. "Thanks, Isabella. But I can't help feeling that there's more to this. I can't shake the feeling that something isn't right."

Isabella nodded in agreement, her captivating dark eyes scanning the room, searching for any signs of deception. "I feel the same way. We need to keep digging, Ethan. There's a deeper layer to all this, and we need to find out what it is."

Ethan nodded, grateful for Isabella's support and understanding. "You're right. Let's continue with the investigation. Are there any updates from you?" he said, determination flashing in his eyes.

"I have a few of my people keeping an eye on my ex-directors' movements. Let's see what happens," she said as she adjusted her skirt.

Ethan noticed her skirt and leaned in towards her to whisper, "You look good in that skirt." Heat rose up in her cheeks; she had not realized how much she craved his attention towards her.

Throughout the day, Isabella and Ethan worked tirelessly, gathering the evidence they needed. Together, they pieced the puzzle together. They couldn't help but feel a growing sense of satisfaction. They were getting closer to exposing the truth. As evening fell, they reconvened in Ethan's study, their hearts pounding with a mixture of excitement and trepidation.

Isabella laid out the evidence she had uncovered, while Ethan shared the connections he had unearthed.

"We're getting closer," Isabella said, her voice tinged with determination.

Ethan nodded, a determined glint in his eyes. "Tomorrow, we'll confront them. We'll show them that we won't back down, no matter how powerful they think they are."

Isabella smiled, feeling a renewed sense of purpose. "Together, we'll bring them to justice," she said.

***

CHAPTER 08: POWER PLAYS AND INTUITION

One evening, after a particularly intense day of investigation, Isabella found herself in the garden of Ethan's mansion. She was taking a moment to catch her breath. Ethan joined her, and they stood side by side, gazing at the stars above.

"I never thought I'd find myself working alongside a billionaire," Isabella remarked. There was a hint of amusement in her voice.

Ethan chuckled. "And I never thought I'd find myself teaming up with my enemy," he replied, his eyes glancing at her with admiration.

Isabella smiled, appreciating the camaraderie they had forged. "You know, we make a pretty good team," she said.

Ethan nodded, his expression serious. "Yes, we do. And I couldn't have asked for a better partner in all this," he admitted, his voice genuine.

Isabella took a deep breath, her eyes meeting Ethan's with a serious expression. "Although I have concrete evidence that Mr. Wilson and Mr. Benson are colluding to bring us down. They've been covering their tracks well. Somehow I managed to uncover some incriminating documents and communication trails. It seems like they were using you and me as pawns in their game. They were trying to manipulate the situation for their gain."

Ethan's jaw clenched as he absorbed the revelation. "I never imagined Mr. Benson could betray me like this. He was like a father figure to me, someone I trusted," he said, his voice tinged with bitterness. "And Mr. Wilson, I always had my doubts about him, but I never thought he would go this far."

Isabella frowned, "You had doubts about Mr. Wilson?"

Ethan sat up straighter and looked right into her

eyes.

"Well, I had to be sure, and so I sent a team to spy on you and Mr. Wilson," he continued, "He was seen multiple times, meeting with Adrian."

Shock coursed through her as she realized that he had known all along. Ethan noticed Isabella's fading smile. "We're in this together, remember? We'll face whatever comes our way, side by side," he assured her.

Isabella nodded, his gaze never leaving hers. "I'm glad you're with me on this journey, Isabella. Your intelligence and determination have been invaluable to me," he admitted. There was a touch of vulnerability in his voice.

Isabella felt her cheeks flush slightly, humbled by his words. "And your resilience and strength have been invaluable to me," she replied.

As they continued to plan their next moves, Isabella knew that their alliance was more than a means to an end. It had evolved into something more profound. It was a connection that transcended the circumstances that had brought them together.

Julianne arrived at Ethan's mansion unannounced. Her confident demeanor filled the room as she made her way to his lounge. Isabella was already present, going through some documents as part of their investigation.

When she saw Julianne, her guard went up. It took her some time to gather her thoughts and realize it was Ethan's step-sister.

"Ah, Ethan, darling brother," Julianne greeted with a saccharine smile, glancing dismissively at Isabella. "I didn't realize you were still keeping company with employees these days."

Ethan's expression tightened at the condescending tone, but he remained composed. "Isabella is not just any employee. She's proven her skills. She's been instrumental in helping me with the current situation."

"Oh, really?" Julianne raised an eyebrow, looking unimpressed. "I hope you're not letting her get too close. We can't have any more unfortunate incidents like Amelia, can we?"

Isabella's jaw tensed, but she refused to let Julianne's jabs get to her. Instead, she chose to focus on her work, knowing the truth about the situation.

Ethan's eyes narrowed, growing wary of Julianne's intentions. "What do you mean by 'unfortunate incidents'?"

Julianne feigned innocence, but her eyes gleamed with mischief. "Oh, you know how Amelia has been getting involved with those shady characters. I don't want to see you hurt again, Ethan."

Isabella was lost. Who was Amelia? What had she and Ethan had in common? Jealousy tinged at her heart, but she knew she had no place to be jealous.

Ethan felt a pang of unease, wondering if there was any truth to Julianne's words. He knew that Amelia had been a wrinkle in his past that still needed to be smoothed out. "I appreciate your concern, Julianne. I can handle my own affairs," Ethan replied. He was trying to defend his ability to make decisions for himself.

Julianne smirked, playing her cards. "Of course, dear brother. I want what's best for you and the family name. After all, we can't let anything tarnish the reputation of the Harringtons." Isabella couldn't help but feel a surge of irritation at Julianne's veiled manipulations.

Before things escalated further, Isabella decided to intervene, addressing Julianne firmly. "Julianne, I understand that you have your concerns. Ethan and I are working together to resolve the situation. You don't need to worry about that."

Julianne turned her icy gaze toward Isabella. "And who are you to tell me what I should or shouldn't worry about? You're a government employee, after all."

Isabella's jaw tightened, but she kept her composure. "I'm someone who cares about Ethan and his well-being. If you have his best interests at heart, you should support him rather than try to undermine him."

Julianne seemed taken aback by Isabella's assertiveness, but she recovered and scoffed. "Well, it's clear you've managed to charm your way into his good graces. I hope you're not after his money."

Ethan's frustration grew, and he stepped in to defend Isabella. "That's enough, Julianne. Isabella is a professional, and she's helping me in a difficult time. I trust her, and that's all that matters."

Isabella appreciated Ethan's support, and she gave him a grateful smile. "Thank you, Ethan. I'll continue to do my best to help you with the investigation."

Julianne huffed, displeased with the turn of

events. "Fine, have it your way. But don't say I didn't warn you," she retorted before turning to leave. As Julianne departed, Isabella let out a sigh of relief. She knew that dealing with Julianne wouldn't be easy. She was determined not to let anyone come between her and her mission to bring the truth to light.

Ethan watched Julianne go, his mind preoccupied with the revelations about Amelia. He knew he couldn't let himself be swayed by Julianne's manipulations. Instead, he turned to Isabella, feeling a newfound sense of trust and reliance on her.

"Thank you for standing up to her," Ethan said, his gaze meeting Isabella's.

Isabella smiled, her resolve strengthening. "I'm here to support you, Ethan. No matter what challenges we face, we'll face them together."

But Ethan's heart was sinking as he absorbed the revelation. Adrian had shared his intimate affairs with Julianne. He felt a mix of anger, betrayal, and embarrassment at the thought of his private moments being exposed, especially with his sister and involving someone like Amelia, whom he had flirted with only once, at an expensive bar.

"How could Adrian do this?" Ethan muttered, clenching his fists in frustration.

He had always trusted Adrian and considered him a close friend and partner. The fact that Adrian had shared such personal details with his step-sister of all people.

Isabella could see the turmoil in Ethan's eyes. She reached out to place a comforting hand on his shoulder. "I'm sorry you had to go through this, Ethan," she said. "It's clear that Adrian is trying to manipulate the situation. He is trying to create discord between you and your sister."

Ethan nodded, trying to collect his thoughts. "I don't understand why he would do this," he admitted. "We've been through so much together, and I thought

I could trust him."

Isabella understood the pain of betrayal, and she spoke with empathy. "Sometimes people show their true colors when faced with difficult situations. It's possible that Adrian is feeling threatened by the investigation. He is trying to protect himself at your expense."

Ethan sighed, feeling torn because of the mounting evidence against him. "I don't want to believe that he's involved in all this," he said, his voice laced with sadness. "But I can't ignore the facts."

Isabella nodded in understanding. "We'll keep digging for the truth, Ethan. Whatever the outcome, you have my support," she assured him.

Ethan appreciated Isabella's support and the strength she provided during this challenging time.

"Thank you, Isabella," he said gratefully. "I don't know how I would get through all this without you."

They shared a moment of silent understanding. The weight of the investigation and the betrayal hung heavy in the air. Despite the uncertainty and the challenges ahead, Ethan felt a sense of relief. He knew he had Isabella by his side. She was not only an intelligent and skilled detective but also a source of reassurance. He had never expected their alliance to develop into something more. As the days went on, he found himself drawn to her in ways he couldn't explain.

***

Ethan would spend his nights deeply immersed in the company's documents and their latest piece of evidence. The night would wear on without taking him with it. Both Ethan and Isabella had been working hard to gather the evidence against the culprits, and he had no other thought on his mind. But things were getting heated outside their world when he received an unknown call one day.

Ethan's phone vibrated with an incoming call from an unknown number. Curious, he picked up the call, not expecting to hear the voice that greeted him.

"Hello? Is this Ethan Harrington?" the caller asked.

"Yes, speaking. May I know who's calling?" Ethan inquired, his curiosity piqued.

"It's Amelia," she said, almost hesitantly.

"Amelia?" Ethan repeated, trying to place the name. Then, it clicked. "Wait, you mean Amelia from the bar, the other day?"

"Yes, that's me," she replied. "I hope you don't mind me calling you out of the blue like this. I had to go through some trouble to find your number."

Ethan's confusion deepened. He remembered the encounter with Amelia at the expensive bar. But it had been a fleeting interaction, and he hadn't thought much about it since then. "No, it's fine. But how did you get my number?" he asked, his curiosity getting the better of him.

"I asked around and did some research," Amelia admitted. "I wanted to talk to you again."

Ethan's brow furrowed. He couldn't fathom why Amelia would go to such lengths to contact him. "Is there something specific you wanted to talk about?" he inquired, trying to sound polite but guarded.

"I wanted to see you again," Amelia said, her voice tinged with a hint of longing. "We had such a great time at the bar, and I couldn't stop thinking about you."

Ethan felt a knot forming in his stomach. He sensed that Amelia's intentions might not be genuine. "Look, I appreciate the sentiment. But I'm in the middle of some important matters right now," he explained, trying to be diplomatic. "I don't think it's a good time for us to meet."

Amelia's tone turned desperate. "Please, Ethan, I want to see you again. I promise I won't take much of your time."

Ethan hesitated, feeling torn between wanting to be polite and not wanting to encourage any unwanted attention. "I'm sorry, but I can't," he said firmly. As he was about to end the call, Amelia interjected, "Wait! There's something you should know. There are people around you who can't be trusted. They are not who they seem to be."

Ethan's curiosity was piqued once again. "What do you mean?" he asked, his voice growing serious.

"I can't say much over the phone, but I have important information that you need to hear in person," Amelia insisted.

Ethan glanced at Isabella, who had been working on her laptop nearby. He wasn't sure if he should take Amelia's words seriously, but the intrigue was undeniable.

"Fine," he finally relented. "We can meet, but it'll

have to be in a public place."

Amelia sounded relieved. "That's perfect! How about the same bar we met last time?"

Ethan hesitated for a moment before agreeing. "Alright, let's meet there in an hour."

As he hung up, a part of him couldn't help but wonder if Amelia's sudden reappearance was a mere coincidence. But deep down, he couldn't help but feel a sense of foreboding about what secrets she might bring to light.

***

As Isabella and Ethan sat together in the living room, the tension in the air was palpable. Isabella couldn't shake the feeling that Ethan was keeping something from her, making her curiosity get the better of her.

"So, who was on the call?" Isabella finally asked,

unable to contain her curiosity any longer.

Ethan hesitated for a moment, avoiding direct eye contact. "Oh, it was someone from work," he replied vaguely.

"Someone from work?" Isabella raised an eyebrow, sensing that he was dodging the question. "You seemed shaken after that call. Are you sure everything is alright?"

Ethan sighed, his mind racing for an excuse that wouldn't reveal too much. "It's some business-related stress, nothing new," he said, hoping to put her worries to rest.

But Isabella was not convinced. She knew there was more to it than work-related stress. "Ethan, we've been through so much together in this investigation. I thought we were a team," she said softly, her eyes searching his face for any hint of the truth.

Ethan looked conflicted, as he was wanting to

protect her from any potential danger. "I know we are a team, Isabella," he replied, his voice sincere. "But this is something I need to handle on my own."

Isabella couldn't help but feel a pang of jealousy. She understood the need for secrecy in certain situations. But a part of her couldn't help but wonder if there was more to it than a work-related issue.

"I trust you, Ethan," she said, her voice tinged with a hint of hurt. "But I can't help but feel left out. We're in this together, aren't we?"

Ethan reached out to take her hand, his expression softening. "Of course we are," he said. "But this is something personal that I need to figure out. I don't want to involve you in any potential danger."

Isabella nodded, understanding his concerns. Yet she couldn't help but feel a sense of frustration. "I get it," she said, trying to hide her emotions. "Just know that I'm here for you if you ever need to talk or if you need my help."

Ethan smiled gratefully, appreciating her support. "Thank you, Isabella. You've been amazing throughout all this," he said.

As the conversation shifted to lighter topics, Isabella tried to push aside her feelings of jealousy. She wanted to focus on the investigation at hand. But in the back of her mind, the questions lingered. She couldn't shake the feeling that there was more to Ethan's secret phone call than he was letting on.

Little did she know that their paths were about to intersect with even more unexpected twists. The bond between them would be tested in ways they never anticipated. Isabella knew that their trust in each other would be crucial in unraveling the truth. In the process, their growing connection would become an even greater source of strength.

As the hour approached for his meeting with Amelia, Ethan found himself torn. He hadn't informed Isabella about the call and his decision to meet her. He believed that it might be dangerous and didn't want to involve Isabella in any potential harm. He respected Isabella's skills as a detective, but he couldn't shake the feeling that this situation required a more personal approach.

When Isabella noticed Ethan's unease, her curiosity was piqued. She couldn't help but feel a tinge of jealousy as she wondered why he was being secretive. Despite her rational mind telling her that he must be meeting with a woman from his past, her heart couldn't help but feel a bit uneasy.

"Is everything alright, Ethan?" Isabella finally asked, unable to hold back her concern any longer.

Ethan tried to put on a reassuring smile. "Yeah, everything's fine. It's a personal matter I need to attend to," he replied.

***

He knew he had to be wary of Amelia's intentions, especially after her unexpected reappearance. Yet, he couldn't shake the memories of their previous encounter at the bar. This only added to his intrigue.

When they finally met at the same bar, Amelia greeted Ethan with a charming smile. "It's so good to see you again, Ethan," she said, her voice dripping with sweetness. "I've been thinking about our time together quite a lot."

Ethan tried to maintain a polite distance. He was reminding himself to stay focused on the reason for the meeting. "Likewise," he replied, keeping his tone neutral. "You mentioned that you have some important information. What is it?"

Amelia leaned in as if sharing a secret. "I've been doing some digging. I found out that there's a massive conspiracy going on within your company," she claimed. Her eyes were sparkling with excitement.

Ethan's curiosity was piqued, but he remained skeptical. "What kind of conspiracy?" he asked, testing the waters.

"Rival companies are plotting to steal your intellectual property," Amelia continued. Her voice was low and enticing. "They've already infiltrated your organization. They are working from within to bring you down."

Ethan's eyes narrowed. It was a dangerous claim, and he couldn't afford to take it lightly. "How do you know all this?" he asked, trying to gauge the authenticity of her information.

Amelia gave him a sly smile. "Let's say I have my sources," she said mysteriously. "But I couldn't keep this information to myself. I knew I had to tell you, Ethan."

As she spoke, Amelia's hand subtly grazed his, and she leaned in even closer. Ethan could feel her trying to win him over. He could tell she was trying to gain his trust, and he couldn't help but feel a mix of discomfort and suspicion.

"Thank you for sharing this with me," Ethan replied, trying to remain composed. "I'll look into it and take the necessary actions."

But Amelia didn't seem satisfied with just providing the information. She continued to flirt with him, trying to appeal to his emotions. "You know, Ethan, we had such a connection the first time we met," she said, her voice low and seductive. "We can pick up where we left off."

Ethan pulled back, his guard up. "I appreciate your concern, Amelia. But I'm dating someone else now," he stated firmly. He did not want to encourage any further advances.

Amelia's smile faded, but she didn't give up that easily. "Well, if things ever change, you know where to find me," she said, her tone still suggestive.

Ethan knew he had to end the conversation before things got any more complicated. "Thank you for your information," he said, standing up. "I'll be in touch if I need anything further."

As he walked away from Amelia, he couldn't help but feel a sense of relief mixed with a tinge of discomfort. He knew he had to be careful not to let her false charm and information cloud his judgment. As he left the bar, he couldn't wait to share everything with Isabella and get her insights on the situation. After all, her intelligence had proven invaluable in navigating their investigation. Together, they were a force to be reckoned with, and Ethan knew he could trust her above anyone else.

Isabella couldn't believe her own eyes as she watched from a distance, hidden in the shadows. Seeing Ethan and Amelia together at the bar, her heart sank as she observed Amelia's hand touching Ethan's. She couldn't help but jump to all the wrong conclusions. Her frustration and jealousy reached a boiling point, and tears welled up in her eyes. She felt a mix of anger and hurt, wondering how Ethan could betray their connection like this. She had grown so close to him during their investigation. She had allowed herself to develop feelings for him that went beyond mere professional admiration.

Seeing him reciprocate Amelia's advances made her feel foolish for letting her guard down. The fear of losing him to someone from his past haunted her. Isabella struggled to control the whirlwind of emotions swirling inside her.

***

CHAPTER 09: TURBULENT PATH

Isabella walked back to her home, her heart heavy with the weight of what she had seen at the bar. She couldn't shake the feeling of hurt and jealousy. Her mind replayed the scene over and over again.

The sight of Ethan getting close to Amelia fueled her insecurities. She had always prided herself on her ability to remain composed and professional. But seeing him with another woman had shattered that facade.

As she reached her doorstep, tears streaming down her cheeks, she was startled to find Ethan standing there. His face had a look of concern and worry. Composing herself as best as she could, she tried to avoid eye contact with him.

"Isabella, are you alright?" Concern etched his face as he stepped towards her.

Isabella walked past him, replying in a hushed

tone. "Why are you here?" As she quickly opened her front door and walked in without hearing his response first, Ethan shook his head and walked in after her, closing the door himself.

Ethan sat on the couch, trying to find the right words to express his feelings to Isabella. Her distant and avoidant demeanor made it difficult for him to open up. He had hoped they could have an honest and heartfelt conversation about what had happened at the bar. It seemed like Isabella was determined to keep her guard up.

"Isabella, can we talk?" he asked, his voice soft with concern.

She looked up from her work, a hint of irritation in her eyes. "Sure, we can talk," she replied, her tone professional and sarcastic.

Ethan felt a pang of frustration but tried to remain patient. "Look, I came to find you because I wanted to talk to you about the investigation. And then I saw you walking in, crying. I am worried about you," he said, trying to convey his genuine concern.

Isabella shrugged nonchalantly. "I'm a grown woman, Ethan. I can take care of myself," she retorted.

He sighed, feeling the distance between them grow even wider. "I know that, Isabella, but I care about you," he said, trying to keep his emotions in check.

She rolled her eyes, not buying into his sentiment. "Well, don't worry about me. I can handle myself fine," she said, her voice tinged with annoyance.

Ethan's frustration grew, and he couldn't help but let it show. "Isabella, can you stop being defensive for once? I'm trying to have a real conversation here," he said, his voice firm.

Her eyes flashed with a mix of surprise and irritation. "Oh, excuse me for being professional and keeping my emotions in check," she shot back.

Unfortunately, her sarcasm was evident.

"That's not what I meant, and you know it," Ethan said, trying to keep his tone calm. "I want to understand what's going on with you. I thought we were partners, that we could talk to each other about anything."

Isabella's expression softened, but she quickly reverted to her defensive stance. "We are partners, Ethan. But that doesn't mean I have to share every little thing with you," she said, her voice guarded.

Ethan felt a twinge of hurt at her words, but he pushed it aside. "I get it, you have your own personal life and that's fine," he said, trying to keep his own emotions in check. "But it feels like you're shutting me out, and I don't know why."

She looked away, avoiding his gaze. "It's easier that way," she mumbled.

"Easier for who?" he asked, his frustration

growing. "For you or for me? Because right now, it feels like you're pushing me away."

Isabella finally looked at him, her eyes guarded but vulnerable. "I don't want to get hurt, Ethan," she admitted. "And sometimes it's easier to keep people at arm's length than to let them in."

He reached out and gently took her hand in his, his touch tender and reassuring. "Isabella, I would never hurt you," he said earnestly. "I care about you, and I want to be there for you."

She tried to pull her hand away, but he held onto it firmly. "You don't know that," she said, her voice wavering. "People change, and they can hurt you without even realizing it."

Ethan felt a pang of sadness at her words. He realized that she must have experienced pain and betrayal in the past. "I can't promise you that I won't make mistakes, Isabella," he said. "But I can promise you that I'll always be honest with you and do my best to be there for you."

Her walls seemed to waver, and he saw a flicker of uncertainty in her eyes. "I need time, Ethan," she said, her voice above a whisper. "I need time to figure things out and to trust myself and my feelings."

Ethan nodded, understanding her need for space. "Take all the time you need," he said. "But know that I'm here whenever you're ready to talk."

As they sat there in silence, he hoped that his words had reached her and that she knew how much he cared about her. But he also knew that he couldn't force her to open up. All he could do was be patient and give her the time and space she needed.

After Ethan left, Isabella found herself alone in her thoughts. Her heart felt heavy with conflicting emotions. She knew she had let her jealousy blind her judgment during the whole incident with Amelia. She also recognized that she had been putting up walls and pushing Ethan away, even though deep down, she cared for him more than she was willing to admit.

As she reflected on the conversation they had, Isabella felt a pang of guilt for being so defensive with him. She knew that Ethan cared about her and was trying to understand her, yet she had shut him out instead of letting him in. The realization made her feel like she had pushed away someone important to her. The truth was, Isabella had never allowed herself to get too close to anyone after the loss of her parents. She had built walls around her heart, afraid of getting hurt again. But now, seeing Ethan's sincerity, she couldn't help but question her own actions.

She recalled the way he had looked at her with concern and how he had held her hand, trying to reassure her. It was a side of him she hadn't seen before, and it made her heart flutter. Isabella knew that she felt something more than a professional connection. But she was scared to admit it to herself.

As the night went on, Isabella found it difficult to focus on anything else. She kept replaying the conversation with Ethan in her mind. She was analyzing every word and every emotion. She realized that her jealousy had clouded her judgment, and she had let her emotions get the best of her. But was it rightful enough of him to act so shady over a meeting with another woman? She felt like there was much more to the picture than what the eye saw.

Ethan couldn't worry about something other than his own company at this stage. But then again, she wondered if she had judged him rightly all along?

In the quietness of her home, Isabella finally allowed herself to admit the truth: she was attracted to Ethan. It was not only physical but emotional as well. The way he confided in her, the way he cared for her, it had all touched her heart in a way she hadn't expected.

But along with her growing feelings for him came fear and uncertainty. She had seen firsthand how betrayal and deceit could ruin everything. She didn't want to put herself in a vulnerable position again. Yet, at the same time, she couldn't deny the connection she felt with Ethan, the way he made her heart race and her mind spin.

***

The drive back to his mansion was filled with thoughts of Isabella that Ethan couldn't shake off. He couldn't help but wonder why she had been acting so strangely lately. The way she had been avoiding eye contact had left him feeling confused and somewhat hurt.

As he drove through the lit streets, he couldn't help but let his mind wander to the possible reasons behind Isabella's behavior. He knew she was a private person and didn't open up about her personal life. But her recent actions seemed to go beyond her usual guarded nature. Ethan considered the possibility that there might be someone else in her life. It could be a boyfriend or someone she was interested in. The thought of Isabella being involved with someone else made him feel a pang of jealousy he hadn't expected.

He clenched his jaw, trying to push away the unwelcome emotions.

"Stop overthinking, Ethan," he muttered to himself, gripping the steering wheel tighter. "It's none of your business. She's her own person, and she doesn't owe you any explanations."

But despite his attempts to rationalize the situation, he couldn't help but feel unsettled. He had grown so used to working with Isabella, and her sudden change in behavior had caught him off guard. As he neared his mansion, Ethan tried to distract himself by focusing on the case. The plans they had made to expose the fraudsters. But the image of Isabella's troubled expression kept intruding into his thoughts. It was making it difficult to concentrate.

He parked his car in the driveway and sat there for a moment, taking a deep breath to calm his racing mind. He knew that he had to respect Isabella's boundaries and not pry into her personal life. But at the same time, he couldn't help but worry that something might be bothering her. It could be something that was unrelated to the case.

With a heavy sigh, Ethan finally got out of the car and made his way inside the mansion. He greeted the butler with a forced smile and went straight to his study. He needed some time alone to clear his head and figure out how to handle his feelings. As he sat behind his desk, Ethan couldn't shake off the feeling of wanting to reach out to Isabella. He wanted to make sure she was okay. But he also knew that it wasn't his place to interfere in her personal life. They were partners, and that was the extent of their relationship.

But despite his rational thoughts, Ethan couldn't help but feel drawn to Isabella in a way he hadn't felt before. He knew that he had to focus on the case and their mission to expose the fraudsters. But at the same time, he couldn't help but hope that Isabella would open up to him and let him in, as he had done with her.

***

Ethan was sitting in his study when James, his butler approached him. He seemed to be in an unusual sense of urgency. He held out a small envelope with no return address, and Ethan could see that it was sealed with an ornate wax stamp.

"Sir, this letter arrived for you just now," James said. His usually composed demeanor seemed flustered. "However, there is no return address on the envelope."

Ethan took the letter, his curiosity piqued by its mysterious appearance. He had received many letters before, but this one felt different. There was an air of secrecy about it that made his heart race. As he opened the envelope and unfolded the letter inside, he found a few lines of puzzling writing. It was like a riddle or a code. The message was enigmatic, leaving him puzzled and concerned.

Subject: A Warning for Your Beloved Detective

Mr. Ethan Harrington,

I trust this message finds you well as you ponder the cryptic words that have come into your possession. You see, I have been observing that the detective, Isabella, has become an integral part of your life.

But let me be clear, Mr. Harrington, your feelings of protectiveness will not shield her from the danger that surrounds her. In fact, she has caught the eye of some very powerful people. Her involvement with you has placed her in their crosshairs.

Your empire now stands on a precipice. The very foundations of your success are about to crumble beneath you. And it is not your empire that is at risk; it is the very life of the detective you hold so dear. I take pleasure in watching your mind race with possibilities. Your empire will fall, and Isabella will find herself trapped in a web of danger from which there is no escape.

You may wonder why I am reaching out to you in such a cryptic manner, and why I choose to keep my identity hidden. The answer is quite simple — I revel in the fear and uncertainty that my presence brings. It is a game, you see, and you are but a mere player, caught in the midst of forces far beyond your comprehension.

As you read these words, know that every move you make is being watched. There is no hiding from the storm that is about to engulf you and your beloved detective. And remember, this is the beginning of a game that you can never hope to win.

Yours cryptically,

A Faceless Adversary

Ethan's brow furrowed as he tried to decipher the mysterious message. It was clear that someone wanted to send him a warning, but the identity of the sender remained a mystery.

"Keep an eye out for any suspicious activity around the mansion," Ethan instructed. "And let me know immediately if anything seems out of the ordinary."

"Yes, sir," James nodded, his concern mirrored in his expression.

As James left the room, Ethan leaned back in his chair, his mind racing with thoughts of the potential threat. He couldn't help but wonder who could be behind this cryptic warning. The feeling of vulnerability and helplessness gnawed at him. He had always been in control of his life and his business.

But now, it seemed like someone was playing a dangerous game, trying to unsettle him and disrupt his plans. But amid the fear and uncertainty, there was also a sense of determination in Ethan. He knew that he couldn't let fear dictate his actions. He had to face the threat head-on and protect those he cared about.

***

The night was dark and quiet as Ethan paced restlessly in his spacious mansion. The cryptic letter had unsettled him. It was the mention of Isabella's name that had sent a surge of distress through his veins. But his growing protectiveness towards her had only intensified. Now he couldn't bear the thought of her being in danger. Unable to stay still, Ethan made a sudden decision. He couldn't wait any longer; he needed to check up on Isabella immediately. He grabbed his car keys and rushed out of the mansion, his heart pounding in his chest.

As he drove through the empty streets, he couldn't shake the feeling of anxiety and worry gnawing at him. He tried calling Isabella many times, but she didn't pick up any of his calls. Each unanswered call heightened his sense of urgency. Arriving at her house, Ethan noticed that all the lights were off. His concern deepened, wondering if she was safe inside. He didn't want to disturb her if she was resting, but he couldn't shake the feeling that something was wrong.

He sent her several text messages, hoping she would see them and respond. 'Isabella, are you there? Please, let me know you're okay. I'm worried about you. Call me back as soon as you can.'

Minutes ticked by like hours, and with each passing moment, Ethan's anxiety grew. He was torn between breaking into her house to ensure her safety and respecting her privacy. But his instincts as a protector and a man who cared for her overpowered his desire to give her space.

Unable to wait any longer, Ethan walked up to her front door and knocked. There was no response. He knocked again, this time a little more insistently, hoping she would hear him. Ethan's heart pounded in his chest as he noticed the broken lock on Isabella's front door. His anxiety escalated, and he knew he couldn't afford to waste any more time. Without hesitation, he reached into his holster and pulled out his gun, clutching it in his hand. He had a feeling that something terrible had happened. He needed to be prepared for whatever he might encounter inside.

The hallway was dimly lit, and the shadows seemed to dance around him as he made his way further into Isabella's home. He called out her name softly, hoping to hear her response, but there was only silence in return. His mind raced with worst-case scenarios, each one more terrifying than the last. He knew he had to stay focused and alert, as he couldn't afford to let his emotions cloud his judgment. He moved, stepping lightly to avoid making any noise. As he reached the living room, his senses heightened.

The room was quiet, and the darkness seemed to envelop everything. He scanned the area, searching for any signs of disturbance or danger. Every creak of the floorboards seemed to echo in his ears, making him even more vigilant.

With his gun raised and senses on high alert, he made his way towards Isabella's bedroom. The door was ajar, and a sliver of light spilled into the hallway. His heart pounded louder in his ears, and he took a deep breath to steady himself before pushing the door open.

Inside, Isabella's room appeared undisturbed. The soft glow of the nightlight illuminated the space, casting shadows on the walls. He searched the room, looking for any signs of an intruder, but everything seemed to be in its place.

His relief was short-lived as he noticed a faint noise coming from the bathroom. He moved towards it, his grip on the gun tightening. The door was ajar, and he could see a faint light filtering through the crack. As he pushed the door open, his breath caught in his throat. There, sitting on the floor, was Isabella, her back pressed against the wall. Her eyes were red from crying, and she looked up at him with a mixture of surprise and relief.

"Ethan," she whispered, her voice shaking with emotion. "I didn't know what to do. They were here, and they threatened me."

Ethan's heart sank as he saw the fear in her eyes. Without a second thought, he holstered his gun and rushed to her side. He pulled her into a comforting embrace. "It's alright, Isabella. You're safe now. I'm here," he assured her, his voice filled with determination and protectiveness.

As Ethan held Isabella in his arms, his protective instincts surged. He was seething with anger at the thought of someone daring to hurt her. He wanted nothing more than to seek out those responsible and make them pay for the fear they had instilled in her.

Yet, he knew that acting on his emotions in that moment wouldn't help Isabella or their situation. Instead, he focused on comforting her. He stroked her hair and whispered reassuring words, trying to calm the storm of emotions that had engulfed her. His own heart was heavy with worry and concern, but he masked his fear to be the strong support Isabella needed.

***

CHAPTER 10: SOLACE IN STORM

Isabella clung to him, finding solace in his presence. "They said they would hurt me if I didn't back off from the investigation. They know about us, Ethan, and they'll stop at nothing to silence me."

In that intimate and vulnerable moment, Ethan realized how much he cared for Isabella. Her safety had become his top priority, and the thought of losing her was unbearable. The fear of the unknown, the faceless threats that lurked in the shadows, made him feel powerless. He wished he could shield her from any harm, but he knew he couldn't erase the dangers that surrounded them.

Despite the fear that gnawed at him, he was determined to face the challenges ahead with her by his side. He saw Isabella not only as a capable detective but also as a person he had grown to cherish and care for. But under his cool composed aura, his anger burned like a wildfire. The mere idea of someone daring to harm her ignited a fury within him that he had never experienced before. Determined to avenge the threats against her, Ethan became laser-focused on unraveling the conspiracy. Every fiber of his being was consumed with the need to bring the culprits to justice, and most of all to ensure that Isabella was safe from harm.

Ethan's heart sank as Isabella recounted the horrifying incident. His anger intensified, yet he tried to keep it in check, focusing instead on being a source of comfort and support for her.

"I can't believe they went after you, Isabella," Ethan said, his voice filled with concern. "Are you okay? Did they hurt you?"

Isabella nodded, wiping away tears as she tried to compose herself. "I'm physically fine, but the fear... it's overwhelming," she admitted, her voice trembling with emotion. "They threatened me, Ethan. They knew about our investigation, and they warned me to stay away or face dire consequences."

Ethan's jaw clenched as he listened, a mix of

emotions swirling inside him. He wanted nothing more than to lash out at those who had threatened Isabella. He knew that now was not the time for recklessness.

"Isabella, you don't have to do this. You don't have to risk your life for this investigation," he said. His voice softened with genuine concern. "We can find another way to handle this. Your safety is my priority."

Tears continued to stream down Isabella's cheeks as she looked into Ethan's eyes. "I can't back down now, Ethan," she said, her voice resolute despite her fear. "I'm in this with you, and I won't let them intimidate me. We need to expose the truth, for the sake of everyone affected by their corruption."

Ethan admired Isabella's courage, but he couldn't help but worry for her safety. He reached out and took her hand in his, offering a comforting squeeze.

"I don't want to see you get hurt, Isabella," he confessed, his voice tinged with vulnerability. "You mean so much to me, and the thought of anything happening to you... it terrifies me."

Isabella looked into his eyes, seeing the genuine concern and care reflected back at her. Her heart swelled with warmth and gratitude for the man standing before her. She knew that her feelings for Ethan had grown far beyond a simple partnership. She also knew that now wasn't the time to explore those emotions.

"I won't let them hurt me, Ethan," she said, mustering her strength, even as the fear still lingered within her. "We'll face this together, like we have been. We're stronger as a team."

Ethan nodded, his grip on her hand tightening. "You're right. We're in this together, no matter what," he said, determination filling his voice. "But promise me that you'll be careful, Isabella. I can't bear the thought of losing you."

Isabella gave him a small, reassuring smile. "I promise," she said. "I'll be careful, and I won't take unnecessary risks. We'll get through this, Ethan. I believe in us."

As the evening drew near, Ethan's concern for Isabella only grew stronger. He knew he couldn't let her stay in her place alone, not after what had happened. He wanted to keep her safe and close to him. So, he offered her a suggestion as they sat on the cozy couch in Isabella's home.

"Isabella, I know it might be too much to ask. I don't want you to be alone tonight," Ethan began, his voice filled with genuine worry. "Why don't you stay with me until we've dealt with this threat? My place has better security, and I can't bear the thought of something happening to you."

Isabella hesitated, touched by Ethan's caring gesture. She appreciated his concern, but she didn't want to impose on him or become a burden.

"I don't want to intrude, Ethan," she replied, trying to maintain a sense of independence. "You've already done so much for me, and I don't want to inconvenience you further."

Ethan shook his head, a gentle smile gracing his lips. "Isabella, it's not an inconvenience at all. I want you to be safe, and I want you here with me," he insisted. "Besides, we're partners in this investigation, and that means we look out for each other."

Isabella's heart swelled with gratitude for his caring nature. She realized that Ethan wasn't looking out for her just as a partner; there was something deeper in his concern. But she couldn't allow herself to get lost in those thoughts. There was too much at stake, and they needed to focus on the task at hand.

"Thank you, Ethan," she said softly, unable to resist the warmth in his eyes. "I appreciate your concern, and I would feel safer here with you. But we must remain focused on our investigation and not let anything distract us."

Ethan nodded, understanding her point. "You're

right. Our priority is exposing the corruption and ensuring justice," he agreed. "But know that I'm here for you, no matter what. If you need anything, don't hesitate to ask."

As they continued their conversation, Ethan prepared a simple dinner for both of them. The atmosphere was filled with an unspoken understanding. There was an unbreakable bond that had formed between them amidst the chaos and danger. They were allies, partners, and perhaps something more.

Ethan insisted on taking care of the cooking. It was a rare sight for someone who was usually occupied with business matters. Isabella watched him move around the kitchen with ease, preparing a meal as if he had been doing it his entire life.

As the aroma of the food filled the air, Isabella couldn't help but feel a mix of emotions. She was touched by Ethan's thoughtfulness and how he seemed to take on the role of caretaker. It was a side of him she hadn't seen before, and it made her heart skip a beat. Isabella found herself mesmerized by the way Ethan's eyes sparkled under the soft glow of the lights. He was more than a billionaire businessman; he was a man with depth, compassion, and vulnerability.

"I hope you like Italian," Ethan said, offering her a plate of pasta. "It's one of the few dishes I know how to make."

Isabella took a bite and couldn't hide the smile that crept onto her lips. "It's delicious," she admitted, savoring the taste. "You're quite the cook."

Ethan chuckled, a hint of pride in his voice. "Well, I have a great teacher," he replied, gesturing towards the kitchen. "My mother used to love cooking, and she taught me a thing or two before she passed away."

Isabella sensed a touch of sadness in his words, and she wanted to reach out and comfort him. She understood the pain of losing loved ones all too well. As they continued their meal, Isabella couldn't help but notice how at ease she felt in Ethan's presence, despite the danger and chaos that surrounded them. There was a sense of calmness whenever they were together. It was as if they could share their fears without judgment or reservation.

"You know," Ethan said, breaking the silence, "I never expected any of this to happen. My life was always about business, power, and ambition. But now, with you by my side, everything feels different."

Isabella looked into his eyes, seeing a depth of emotion that mirrored her own. "I feel the same way," she admitted, her voice soft. "Being with you has made me see things differently too. I never thought I'd find someone who understands me on this level."

Ethan smiled warmly at her, taking another bite of the delicious pasta he had cooked in her kitchen.

After dinner, they settled into the living room. Ethan spoke again, his voice filled with genuine worry. "I'll try to convince you again. Let's go to my place. If

I leave you here alone, I'll probably spend the night worrying."

Isabella hesitated, touched by Ethan's caring gesture. She appreciated his concern, but she didn't want to impose on him or become a burden. She also remembered the rude words of his stepsister, Julianne.

"I don't want to intrude, Ethan," she replied, trying to maintain a sense of independence. "You've already done so much for me, and I don't want to inconvenience you further."

Ethan shook his head, a gentle smile gracing his lips. "Isabella, it's not an inconvenience at all. I want you to be safe, and I want you here with me," he insisted.

"Thank you, Ethan," she said softly, unable to resist the warmth in his eyes. "I'll stay at your place."

Yet, as the night grew darker, she knew she had to be cautious with her emotions. There were still secrets and dangers lurking. She couldn't afford to let her feelings cloud her judgment.

Soon, they were discussing their plans for the following day. Ethan's arm casually draped over the back of the couch, a silent invitation for Isabella to lean in closer.

The temptation to feel his reassuring presence was strong, but she maintained a professional distance. As the clock ticked on, Ethan couldn't ignore the undeniable connection he felt with Isabella. He wanted to protect her, not just as a partner, but as something more profound. However, he also understood that the timing was delicate. They had to navigate the dangers that surrounded them.

Isabella's heart felt conflicted as she tried to comprehend the depth of her emotions. She had always been self-reliant, used to taking care of herself and others. But now, with Ethan's gestures of kindness, she found herself yearning for something more. It was a delicate balance between wanting to remain strong and independent.

***

Ethan's voice broke through her thoughts, bringing her back to the present moment as they sat in the car. "It won't take long, Isabella," he said with a reassuring smile, having noticed her contemplative expression, "relax and let me take care of you for a change."

Isabella nodded lightly, unable to find the right words to express the whirlwind of emotions within her. With each passing moment, Isabella's walls were crumbling. She found herself wanting to trust Ethan with her vulnerabilities.

There was something about him that made her feel safe, despite the dangers that surrounded them. It was as if he could see through her defenses and was willing to stand by her side no matter what.

The drive back to Ethan's mansion was a quiet

one. The weight of the day's events still lingered in the air, and there was an unspoken understanding between them. Isabella sat in the passenger seat, her thoughts a whirlwind of emotions, stealing glances at Ethan from time to time.

Ethan's grip on the steering wheel tightened as they navigated through the streets. He couldn't shake the feeling of relief that coursed through him. He knew that Isabella was safe with him. He glanced at her, seeing the exhaustion in her eyes, and he wished he could do more to ease her burden.

"I'm glad you came with me," Ethan finally spoke, breaking the silence. "I couldn't bear the thought of leaving you alone tonight."

Isabella smiled softly, the gesture reaching her tired eyes. "Thank you, Ethan. I don't know what I would've done if you hadn't been there."

He gave her a reassuring nod. "We're in this together, Isabella. I won't let anything happen to you."

The weight of his words settled in, and Isabella felt a mixture of gratitude. It was becoming harder for her to ignore the growing attraction. As they pulled up to the mansion, the grandeur of the building was an impressive sight. Ethan's butler, James, opened the door for them, and they made their way inside. Isabella marveled at the opulence of the place but also felt a sense of comfort in the warmth of its walls.

Ethan led her to a cozy sitting room, away from the prying eyes of the staff. "You should rest here for the night," he said, motioning to the plush sofa. "I'll have James prepare the guest room for you."

Isabella hesitated, feeling a mix of gratefulness and guilt. "I don't want to intrude, Ethan. You've already done so much for me."

He shook his head, a determined look in his eyes. "Nonsense. You're not intruding at all. I want you to feel safe here, Isabella. Please, stay." She relented, unable to resist the sincerity in his voice. "Thank you, Ethan. I appreciate it."

As James prepared the guest room, Isabella found herself drawn to Ethan's presence.

Once the guest room was ready, Ethan escorted her there. Isabella couldn't help but feel a sense of vulnerability as she followed him. She knew she was teetering on the edge of something unknown, and the pull towards him was undeniable.

In the dimly lit room, Ethan paused before her, his eyes searching hers. "If you need anything, anything at all, don't hesitate to ask," he said.

Isabella nodded, feeling her heart flutter in her chest. "I will. Thank you, Ethan, for everything."

As he turned to leave, Isabella's hand reached out to grasp his arm. This was also surprising for herself with the gesture. He turned back to face her, their eyes locking, and she felt the electricity between them once more.

"Stay with me," she blurted out, the words leaving

her lips before she could stop herself. "I mean, not just for tonight, but... I don't want to face this alone."

Ethan's expression softened, and a glimmer of understanding passed between them. Without a word, he pulled her into his arms, and Isabella found herself wrapped in his warmth and comfort.

"You don't have to face anything alone, Isabella," he whispered. "I'm here, and I'll be here for as long as you need me."

In that moment, Isabella knew that she had found someone she could trust and rely on. Despite the dangers and uncertainties that lay ahead, she felt a sense of peace in Ethan's arms. And as they held each other, she knew that their paths had been destined to intertwine. It was leading them to this moment of solace and understanding.

In the soft glow of the moonlight filtering through the curtains, Isabella looked up at Ethan. Her heart full of gratitude and a hint of vulnerability. "Ethan, I don't even know what to say," she admitted, her voice trembling. "You've done so much for me, and I can't believe how much you care."

Ethan cupped her face in his hands, his gaze unwavering. "Isabella, I meant what I said earlier. I won't let anything happen to you. I'll find out who's behind all this, and I'll make sure they pay for what they've done. You have my word."

She felt a rush of emotions wash over her. There was relief, trust, and something else she hadn't allowed herself to feel until now. "Thank you," she whispered, a single tear escaping her eye. "I never thought I would find someone like you, someone who cares."

Ethan's thumb brushed away the tear, and a warm smile graced his lips. "I care about you more than I can put into words, Isabella. From the moment we met, you've challenged me and intrigued me. You've brought light into my life when all seemed dark."

Isabella's heart skipped a beat, and she swallowed

the lump in her throat. "But... we're in the middle of an investigation. I can't let my feelings cloud my judgment," she said, trying to regain her composure.

Ethan shook his head, a determined glint in his eyes. "I know, Isabella, but that doesn't mean we have to ignore what we feel. I won't let anything come between us, not even this investigation. We'll face this together, as a team."

Her heart fluttered at his words, and she couldn't help but be drawn to the sincerity in his eyes. "I've never felt this way before," she confessed, her voice above a whisper.

"Neither have I," Ethan admitted, his thumb caressing her cheek. "But sometimes, life throws unexpected challenges our way. We have to be brave enough to face them head-on. And I know I want to face them with you by my side." Isabella felt the fear of the unknown, and excitement all at once. With Ethan, she felt safe, understood, and cared for in a way she had never experienced before.

"You're an incredible person, Isabella," Ethan said. "And I can't imagine my life without you in it. No matter what happens, I want you to know that I'm here for you, and I care for you."

A tear of overwhelming emotion escaped Isabella's eye. She leaned into Ethan's touch, finding comfort in his presence. "I care about you too, Ethan," she finally admitted, her voice raw with emotion. "And I want to face this together, as a team."

In that moment, they both knew that they were bound not only by the investigation but by something deeper. It was a connection that defied logic and reason. They knew that no matter what the future held, they had found something precious.

A love that would weather any storm and stand strong against the trials that lay ahead. With their hearts aligned and their commitment to justice unwavering, they were ready to face whatever came their way. Together, they would expose the web of corruption, bring the culprits to justice. And as Ethan looked at

Isabella, he knew that no matter what happened, they would emerge stronger than ever before.

***

CHAPTER 11: TRUST UNDER FIRE

As the clock struck midnight, he decided it was time to talk to Isabella about everything. He couldn't bear the thought of her being in the dark about the potential dangers they were facing. He wanted her to be prepared and vigilant, as he was. He was determined to protect Isabella at all costs, and he knew that the time for action was near. The threats against her had only fueled his resolve to bring down the perpetrators responsible for endangering her life.

"Isabella, there's something I need to tell you," he began, his voice steady but his heart racing.

She nodded, inviting him into her room. "What is it, Ethan?"

He took a deep breath, choosing his words carefully. "I received a mysterious letter today. It was a warning, a threat against both of us."

Isabella's eyes widened, and she moved closer to

him. "A threat? What did it say?"

"It mentioned that you were in danger and that my empire would crumble in the coming days," Ethan explained. He didn't want to hide anything from her.

Isabella's hand instinctively reached for his, seeking comfort and reassurance. "We can't let this scare us, Ethan. We need to face this together, like we've been doing all along."

He squeezed her hand, grateful for her unwavering support. "You're right. We can't back down now. The truth needs to come out, and those responsible must be held accountable."

Isabella nodded, her eyes determined. "I agree, Ethan. We've come too far to turn back now. We have to expose the truth and put an end to this corruption once and for all."

Ethan felt a rush of admiration for Isabella's courage and resolve. She was fearless in the face of danger, and he knew he could trust her completely. "I couldn't have asked for a better partner in this, Isabella. Your intelligence and dedication to this case have been invaluable."

She smiled, her hand still clasped in his. "Thank you, Ethan. The feeling is mutual. Together, we can make a difference and bring justice to those who have tried to harm us."

Ethan took a deep breath, knowing that what he was about to suggest would be risky.

But it was a risk they needed to take to bring down the powerful enemies they were up against. "There's one final move we can make to expose the culprits and gather enough evidence to bring them down. It's risky, and we might lose some things along the way, but it's the only way to get to the truth."

Isabella looked at him with unwavering trust in her eyes. "Tell me what we need to do, Ethan. I'm ready to do whatever it takes."

"We need to host a grand unveiling. Like a press conference where we lay out all the evidence we've gathered," Ethan explained. "We'll reveal the entire web of corruption. Starting from the highest levels of government to the heart of the pharmaceutical industry. It's our final blow, and it'll be a dangerous game, but it's the only way to expose them."

Isabella nodded, understanding the gravity of their decision. "It's risky, but if we can manage to pull it off, it'll be worth it. We have to show the world the truth and let them decide for themselves."

Ethan smiled, feeling a sense of relief that Isabella was on board with the plan. "Exactly. We can't let fear hold us back. We need to have faith in the justice system and the people's judgment."

She squeezed his hand reassuringly. "I have faith in you, Ethan. I know we can do this together."

As they stood there, hand in hand, they both knew that the road ahead would be challenging and dangerous. But they also knew that they had each other's backs, and that gave them the strength to face whatever came their way.

"We'll prepare everything for the press conference," Isabella said. There was determination shining in her eyes. "Let's make sure we have all the evidence we need to back up our claims."

Ethan nodded, a sense of purpose filling him. "We'll expose them for what they are, and we won't let anything stand in our way."

As they embraced each other, they knew that their final blow would be their most significant yet. It was a risk they were willing to take to bring the truth to light. They wanted to put an end to the corruption that had threatened their lives and their world. With their resolve strengthened, they set out to prepare for the press conference that would change everything. The stakes were high, but they knew that together, they were an unstoppable force. And as they embarked on this perilous journey, they had one another to lean on, and that made all the difference.

***

Ethan and Isabella were well aware that their battle against corruption would not be easy. They gathered evidence and prepared to expose the culprits. But they knew that legal roadblocks were a very real possibility. Their fears were confirmed the next morning when they received a letter from a powerful law firm representing the interests of those involved in the corruption.

The letter accused Ethan and Isabella of spreading false information and making baseless allegations against their clients. It threatened legal action if they did not immediately halt their investigation.

"This is exactly what we were afraid of," Isabella said, frustration evident in her voice.

"They're trying to scare us into backing down," Ethan clenched his jaw, his determination only growing stronger. "We can't let them intimidate us," he replied. "We have a duty to expose the truth, no matter what obstacles they throw our way."

***

Later that day, the atmosphere in the conference room was tense as Ethan, Isabella, and their team gathered around a large wooden table. The letter from the powerful law firm lay in the center, its menacing words a stark reminder of the uphill battle they faced in their pursuit of justice.

Isabella broke the silence with her voice determined, "We can't let this letter intimidate us. We knew they would try to throw legal hurdles our way. We need to stay focused and strong."

Ethan nodded, his jaw set with determination. "We won't back down. The evidence we've uncovered is real, and we have a duty to bring the truth to light."

Jake, one of their team members, chimed in,

"They're trying to use fear to stop us, but we can't let them. We have the law on our side, and we'll fight back with everything we've got."

Isabella nodded, her resolve matching his. "You're right. We need to be prepared for a legal battle. We'll need a strong legal team on our side." They wasted no time in seeking the best legal representation they could find. They hired a team of experienced lawyers who were not swayed by the threats.

But, as they moved forward, they found themselves faced with a barrage of lawsuits. They were using their influence to discredit Isabella's reputation as a detective. By painting her as an untrustworthy individual, they tried to shatter Ethan's trust.

Isabella felt the weight of the attacks on her personal and professional integrity. It hurt to see her dedication and hard work being undermined and questioned. But she refused to let it deter her. Instead, she used the legal challenges as motivation to uncover even more evidence. Ethan, too, faced his own share of legal battles. False reports about his company were circulated. There were attempts to damage his reputation as a successful entrepreneur. The stress of the situation was immense. But he drew strength from Isabella's unwavering support. Amidst the legal turmoil, Ethan and Isabella leaned on each other. They found comfort and strength in their partnership. Their bond deepened as they navigated the storm together, facing the challenges head-on.

***

The meeting room was somber. The air thick with tension as Ethan and Adrian faced each other across the polished table. Ethan's eyes were fixed on Adrian, searching for any sign of the friend he once knew. But the man before him now seemed different, colder, and driven by ulterior motives.

"I've heard about the allegations against the company, Ethan," Adrian began. His voice was laced with a hint of condescension. "This investigation of yours is causing a lot of trouble. You need to put an end to it."

Ethan's jaw tightened, and he responded, "I can't do that, Adrian. The allegations are serious, and we need to get to the truth. I won't back down."

Adrian leaned back in his chair, a sly smile playing on his lips. "Think carefully, Ethan. If you continue down this path, it could ruin the company. And I won't stand by and watch that happen."

Ethan's eyes narrowed, his resolve unwavering. "Are you threatening me, Adrian?"

Adrian's smile grew wider, "Consider it more of a friendly warning. I don't want to see you ruin everything you've built. Stop this investigation, and we can work together to protect the company."

Ethan's grip on the edge of the table tightened. He had trusted Adrian, but now he saw a side of him that he had never suspected. "I can't believe you're asking me to give up on seeking the truth."

Adrian's tone turned icy, "The truth doesn't always matter, Ethan. What matters is the reputation of the company and my position in it."

Ethan shook his head in disbelief, "So, it's all about power and control for you?"

Adrian's eyes flashed with a hint of anger, "You wouldn't understand, Ethan. You've always had everything handed to you on a silver platter. You don't know what it's like to work your way up from nothing."

Ethan's face hardened, "You know nothing about me, Adrian. I've worked hard to build this company, and I won't let anyone destroy it, not even you."

Adrian's smile vanished, replaced by a steely expression. "Well, if you won't listen to reason, then I have no choice but to take matters into my own hands."

Ethan's heart sank as he realized the depth of Adrian's betrayal. "Are you threatening to leave the company?"

Adrian nodded, his eyes unwavering, "I'll do whatever it takes to protect what's mine, Ethan. And if you won't cooperate, then I'll find someone who will."

The room fell silent as the weight of Adrian's ultimatum hung in the air. Ethan knew he couldn't let Adrian's greed dictate the course of his investigation. He had to stand firm and continue the fight for justice, even if it meant losing someone he once considered a friend.

With a heavy heart, Ethan stood up, his voice steady, "I won't be blackmailed, Adrian. I'll do what's right, no matter the consequences."

Adrian's eyes narrowed, "Then you leave me with no choice."

As Ethan left the room, he knew that the relationship between him and Adrian had changed irreversibly. The once-solid bond of friendship had been shattered, replaced by a bitter rivalry driven by power and deceit.

At that moment, Ethan resolved to expose the truth, no matter the cost. He would face the allegations head-on and bring the culprits to justice. He didn't care if it meant going against those he once trusted. The battle for the truth had intensified. Ethan was ready to face whatever obstacles lay ahead.

***

Isabella was seated at her desk, engrossed in reviewing some documents when she heard a knock on her office door. She looked up to see Amelia standing there, a sly smile playing on her lips.

"Well, well, if it isn't the detective herself," Amelia said, her voice dripping with arrogance. "I must say, I'm surprised to see you still hanging around Ethan. I thought you would have given up by now."

Isabella raised an eyebrow, unfazed by Amelia's

taunts. "What do you want, Amelia?"

Amelia took a step closer, her eyes narrowing. "I want you to stay away from Ethan. He's mine, and I won't let some detective like you ruin what we have."

Isabella couldn't help but scoff. "What you have with Ethan is nothing more than a fling. He's not interested in you, Amelia."

Amelia's smile wavered for a moment, but she regained her composure. "Oh, I think you're wrong about that. Ethan and I have a connection that you can never understand."

Isabella leaned back in her chair, her expression unyielding. "Save your theatrics, Amelia. I know what you're trying to do. You're trying to manipulate me into leaving Ethan, but it's not going to work."

Amelia's eyes flashed with anger, and she took a step even closer to Isabella. "You think you're so smart, don't you? But let me tell you something. Ethan will never choose you over me. He may be intrigued by your little investigation, but he'll come running back to me in the end."

Isabella felt a surge of irritation at Amelia's arrogance. "You seem awfully confident about that. But let me remind you that I've known Ethan longer than you have. I know him better than you do."

Amelia laughed mockingly. "Oh, please. What do you know about him? You're a detective, trying to dig up dirt on him and his company. You think he would choose you over someone like me?"

Isabella clenched her fists, trying to keep her cool. "This is not a competition, Amelia. I care about Ethan, and I won't let anyone, including you, manipulate him."

Amelia's smile turned sinister. "Well, then you're in for a rude awakening, detective. You have no chance with Ethan. He's too good for the likes of you."

Isabella felt a pang of hurt at Amelia's words, but

she refused to show it. "We'll see about that," she said, her voice steady. "Ethan is a smart man, and he can see through your games."

Amelia scoffed, turning to leave. "We'll see indeed. But mark my words, detective. You'll regret getting involved with Ethan."

As Amelia walked out of the office, Isabella took a deep breath, trying to calm her racing heart. She knew Amelia was trying to get under her skin, but her words had hit a nerve. The encounter had left Isabella feeling unsettled. She couldn't shake the feeling that there was something suspicious about Amelia's actions.

But as she thought about Ethan, she felt a sense of reassurance. Despite Amelia's threats, Ethan had shown nothing but care and concern for her. He had stood by her side during the most difficult moments. Isabella knew that their bond was stronger than any petty games

Amelia might play. She wouldn't let Amelia or

anyone else stand in her way, especially when it came to protecting the man she cared about deeply.

Isabella couldn't shake off the unsettling encounter with Amelia. As the days passed, she felt a growing need to confront Ethan about the matter. She knew that keeping it to herself would only create more misunderstandings between them.

So, one evening, she mustered up the courage to have a candid conversation with him.

As they sat in the living room of his mansion, Isabella took a deep breath and decided to broach the subject. "Ethan, there's something I need to talk to you about," she began, her eyes meeting his with determination.

Ethan looked at her, concern evident in his eyes. "Of course, Isabella. What's bothering you?"

"Amelia came to 'threaten' me a few days ago," she said, her voice steady. "She came to my office and tried to manipulate me, saying that she and you have some sort of connection."

Ethan sighed, running a hand through his hair. "I see. Look, Isabella, I should have told you about Amelia before. We met at a bar and yes, we flirted a little. But that's all there was to it. It's over now, and she's trying to use that to her advantage."

Isabella nodded, taking in his words. "I needed to hear it from you, Ethan. I didn't want to jump to conclusions, but her words had me worried."

"I understand," Ethan said. "And I'm sorry if it caused you any distress. But I want to assure you that there's nothing between Amelia and me. I'm only partly entertaining her antics, just in case she might reveal something useful for our investigation."

Isabella felt a mixture of relief and reassurance hearing his explanation. "Thank you for being honest with me," she said sincerely. "I trust you, Ethan, and I know that you wouldn't let anyone come between us."

He smiled, his eyes softening. "I feel the same way about you, Isabella. You mean a lot to me, and I wouldn't let anything or anyone jeopardize what we have." Their eyes locked in a moment of understanding. Isabella felt a warmth spreading through her. She knew that Ethan was being sincere, and she couldn't help but feel a surge of affection for him.

"I'm glad we talked about this," Isabella said, her voice soft. "I don't want anything to come between us, especially not someone like Amelia."

Ethan reached out and took her hand in his. "You don't have to worry, Isabella. I'm committed to you and to finding the truth together. We'll get through this, like we've gotten through everything else."

Isabella smiled, her heart swelling with affection for him. "I believe in us, Ethan. We're a team, and together, we can overcome any obstacle."

He squeezed her hand, his eyes never leaving hers.

"That's the spirit. We'll face whatever comes our way, and we'll come out stronger on the other side."

***

"Enough is enough," Adrian sneered, his eyes glinting with malice. "Ethan Harrington has become a thorn in our side for far too long. He's too stubborn to back down, even in the face of threats. It's time we take more drastic measures."

Adrian sat at the head of a large table, surrounded by his nefarious teammates. The air was heavy with tension and malice as they plotted their next move.

They were determined to get rid of Ethan, who had become an insurmountable obstacle in their path. His teammates nodded in agreement, their expressions cold and calculating. They were all united in their desire to protect their secrets. They would go to any lengths to prevent Ethan from exposing the truth to the world.

"He's proven to be more resilient than we

anticipated," one of the team members said. His voice was laced with frustration. "Our attempts to discredit him and Isabella haven't worked as we hoped."

"We can't let them ruin everything we've worked so hard to build," another teammate chimed in. "It's time to cut out the problem once and for all."

Adrian leaned back in his chair, a sinister grin spreading across his face. "Yes, it's time to make a statement. We need to show Ethan Harrington that he can't mess with us and get away with it."

His teammates exchanged dark glances, their minds already concocting a sinister plan. They were ready to do whatever it took to protect their interests.

"We need to be careful," another team member warned. "We can't afford any mistakes or tracebacks to us."

Adrian nodded, his eyes gleaming with determination. "Don't worry; I've already taken care of everything. We'll make it look like an accident, and no one will suspect a thing."

***

CHAPTER 12: UNMASKING THE CULPRITS

In the weeks leading up to the court hearing, Isabella and Ethan worked tirelessly. They gathered evidence, planned, and prepared for their grand unveiling. The courtroom was packed with reporters, lawyers, and curious onlookers. They were all eager to witness the high-stakes trial. As they stood side by side, Isabella could feel Ethan's nervous energy radiating from him. He was determined to expose the truth. But the weight of the responsibility was evident in his tense shoulders.

"Are you ready for this?" Isabella whispered, trying to offer some reassurance.

Ethan nodded, his jaw clenched. "As ready as I'll ever be. We have to do this, Isabella. It's the only way to stop them and bring justice."

Their lawyer, a trusted ally in their fight for justice, approached them with a confident smile. "We've got a strong case, Mr. Harrington. We'll start by exposing the minor players first. This is to build momentum and set the stage for the bigger revelations."

Ethan nodded again, taking a deep breath to steady himself. "Let's do it. Let's bring them down."

The court proceedings began, and their lawyer meticulously presented the evidence. Their first victim was Mr. Benson and the other minor culprits. Emails, financial records, and witness testimonies were laid out, painting a damning picture of their fraudulent schemes and illegal activities.

Ethan sat tall, his eyes fixed on the defendants as their guilt was revealed to the world. He felt a sense of satisfaction knowing that he was finally putting an end to their deceitful ways.

As each piece of evidence was presented, Isabella saw a fire ignite in Ethan's eyes. His determination to expose the truth was unwavering. She couldn't help but feel a surge of admiration for him. "You've done a great job," Isabella whispered, giving him a supportive squeeze on the arm.

He turned to her, a small smile playing on his lips. "We're just getting started."

Soon all the minor culprits were exposed. Now it was time for a short recess before they moved on to the bigger revelations. Isabella and Ethan retreated to a quiet corner of the courthouse where they could briefly discuss their next steps.

"You did amazing in there," Isabella praised, her heart swelling with pride for him.

Ethan's eyes softened as he looked at her. "I couldn't have done it without you, Isabella. You've been my rock throughout all this."

She smiled warmly at him, appreciating his words. "We make a good team."

The recess ended, and they returned to the

courtroom. As the trial resumed, the tension in the air grew palpable. Isabella could feel the weight of the moment as they prepared to expose the bigger culprits.

Their lawyer took the stage once again. Isabella watched as Ethan's hands clenched into fists, and she knew he was ready to take them down. With each revelation, the courtroom erupted into gasps and murmurs. The evidence was overwhelming, leaving no room for doubt. As the truth unraveled before them, Isabella noticed the horrified expressions on the faces of those who had once trusted Adrian and Mr. Benson. Their empire of lies was crumbling, and they were left exposed and vulnerable.

Isabella stood by Ethan's side, feeling a mix of emotions. The satisfaction of justice being served was tinged with sadness. But she knew that they were doing the right thing, and that gave her the strength to continue. As the court hearing continued, Isabella and Ethan were determined to see it through to the end. They knew that their fight for justice was far from over. They were ready to face whatever challenges lay ahead.

Together, they would expose the truth and bring down the corrupt empire that had once threatened to destroy them both.

Murmurs of disbelief and nervous whispers spread among them as they realized the gravity of the situation. Adrian, in particular, seemed to be growing desperate. His face turned pale. Beads of sweat formed on his forehead as he saw his empire of lies unraveling before his eyes. He exchanged worried glances with Mr. Benson, who looked distressed.

Mr. Benson, who had once been a pillar of confidence, now found himself on the receiving end of accusations. It was like he had never expected to face the consequences of his actions. His arrogance waned, and he became uncomfortable. All his attempts to defend himself fell flat against the mounting evidence.

As the trial continued, the opposing party's lawyer attempted to discredit the evidence presented by Isabella and Ethan's team. But their arguments seemed feeble in comparison to the concrete proof brought forth. Isabella's skillful cross-examinations left the defense struggling to come up with reasonable explanations. Amidst the chaos, Adrian attempted to maintain a facade of control, but his eyes betrayed his fear. He knew that his constructed empire was crumbling, and he was running out of options to salvage it.

With a determined glint in his eyes, Ethan stood tall and resolute. He was ready to face whatever challenges lay ahead, and he was not going to back down. Isabella stood by his side, her unwavering support giving him the strength to see this through to the end.

***

The judge addressed the packed courtroom. His voice was firm yet impartial. "Ladies and gentlemen, we have heard the arguments and evidence presented by both parties in this court hearing."

"While the evidence brought forth by Mr. Ethan

Harrington's side is indeed compelling, the court acknowledges that some aspects may still need further scrutiny to arrive at a conclusion."

A hushed murmur swept through the courtroom as the judge's words hung in the air. Isabella and Ethan exchanged glances, feeling a mixture of relief and anticipation. They had come so far in exposing the truth, and now it seemed they were on the cusp of achieving justice.

The judge continued, "In the interest of ensuring a fair and thorough examination of the evidence, this court has decided to adjourn the proceedings to another hearing within a week. During this time, both parties are encouraged to provide any more evidence."

Isabella's heart skipped a beat, and she swallowed the lump in her throat. The realization that their victory was not yet absolute hit her hard.

She knew they had to stay focused and diligent in preparing for the final battle.

The judge's gaze settled on Isabella and Ethan, and he addressed them. "Mr. Harrington, Detective Knight, I must commend you for bringing to light the serious evidence of corruption. But, as this matter involves significant implications, it is imperative that we proceed with caution to ensure a fair judgment."

"We understand, Your Honor," Isabella replied. Her voice was steady despite the swirl of emotions within her. "We will use this time to bolster our evidence and address any questions the court may have."

The judge nodded in approval. "Very well. I trust that both parties will act responsibly. We will reconvene in one week to reach a final decision."

As the courtroom began to disperse, Isabella and Ethan retreated back to their cars. The weight of the victory still hung in the air as they both took a moment to process the events of the day.

Their eyes met, and they shared a silent nod of

understanding, knowing that their fight was far from over.

***

Isabella opened the door to the car and turned to Ethan, her expression a mix of relief and determination. "We did it," she said, her voice tinged with emotion. "We actually did it."

Ethan smiled, a genuine sense of pride shining in his eyes. "Yes, we did," he replied. "And it's all thanks to your unwavering dedication and brilliance. I couldn't have asked for a better partner in this fight."

Isabella blushed at the compliment, but she knew that they had truly been a formidable team. "It was a team effort," she said. "We both brought our strengths to the table, and together, we were able to expose the truth."

Ethan nodded in agreement. "You're right," he said. "I'm grateful to have you by my side throughout all this."

As they stood there, a comfortable silence settled between them. Isabella glanced around, the reality of the victory sinking in. But she also knew that they couldn't afford to let their guard down just yet.

"We need to stay vigilant," she said, breaking the silence. "The culprits won't give up easily, and they may try to retaliate."

Ethan's expression turned serious, the weight of responsibility settling back onto his shoulders. "You're right," he said. "We can't let our guard down. We need to be prepared for whatever they throw at us next."

Isabella took a deep breath, knowing that their battle was far from over. "We should also be careful about our communications," she suggested. "We know they might try to intercept or watch our conversations."

Ethan nodded in agreement. "I'll have my IT team

beef up our security measures," he said. "We can't afford any leaks or vulnerabilities."

As they discussed their next steps, Isabella couldn't help but feel a sense of admiration for Ethan. Despite the challenges they had faced, Ethan would remain resolute and determined to see this fight through to the end.

"I'm proud of you, Ethan," she said, her voice soft but sincere. "You could have given in to their threats, but you chose to stand up for what's right."

Ethan smiled, a touch of vulnerability in his eyes. "I couldn't let them win," he said. "Not after everything they've done."

Isabella reached out and placed a reassuring hand on his arm. "We'll get through this," she said. "Together."

Ethan nodded, grateful for her support. "Together," he echoed.

Over the course of days, Isabella and Ethan worked to shore up their case and prepare for the final showdown.

They were met with more challenges and obstacles, and they faced each one head-on, determined to see justice served.

One evening, as they sat in Ethan's office, Isabella couldn't help but voice her admiration. "You never give up, do you?" she said, a hint of awe in her voice.

Ethan chuckled, but there was a hint of weariness in his eyes. "I can't afford to," he said. "Not when so much is at stake."

Isabella nodded in understanding, but she also knew that he was carrying a heavy burden. "You don't have to do this alone, you know," she said gently. "I'm here for you, every step of the way."

Ethan looked at her. There was gratitude shining in his eyes. "I know," he said. "And I'm grateful for that."

***

Ethan sat behind his imposing desk. His face bore a mask of controlled determination as he stared at the papers spread out in front of him. He had been expecting this confrontation, but that didn't make it any less tense. The door to his office swung open. Adrian strode in, his usually confident demeanor marred by a hint of unease.

"Adrian," Ethan acknowledged coolly. His tone was a stark contrast to the warmth they had once shared.

"Ethan," Adrian replied, his voice tinged with a mixture of resignation and defiance. "We need to talk."

Ethan gestured to the chair opposite him. "By all means, have a seat."

Adrian sank into the chair, his fingers tapping

nervously on the armrest. "I've been thinking, Ethan. This whole situation has become a nightmare. The allegations, the media scrutiny—it's all too much. I can't handle it anymore."

Ethan leaned back, studying Adrian. "So, you've come to resign?"

Adrian nodded, his jaw clenched. "Yes, that's what I've decided. I can't let my association with your company destroy my own reputation."

Ethan's gaze hardened, a glint of skepticism in his eyes. "And what about your loyalty? Your loyalty to this company and to me?"

Adrian's gaze wavered, guilt flickering across his features. "Ethan, you have to understand—"

Ethan's voice turned steely. "Understand what, Adrian? That you're willing to abandon ship when the waters get rough? When we're on the brink of exposing the truth?"

Adrian's eyes flashed, a hint of defensiveness creeping into his tone. "I've done everything I could, Ethan. But this battle is too intense. I have a family to think about, a future to secure."

Ethan's fists clenched beneath the desk, his frustration palpable. "And what about the reputation of my family? What about the future of this company, the livelihoods of countless employees? Are you willing to walk away from all that?"

Adrian's expression darkened, a spark of resentment igniting. "You have no idea what it's like, Ethan. To be in my position, to bear the weight of this company on your shoulders."

Ethan's voice dropped to a dangerous whisper. "I know exactly what it's like, Adrian. I've carried this burden since day one, and I've never shied away from it. I've fought tooth and nail to protect what my father built. Just to ensure that his legacy isn't tarnished by greed and corruption."

Adrian's gaze held a mixture of frustration and defensiveness. "You're relentless, Ethan. It's like you're on a crusade to save the world. But I can't keep up with your pace. I won't be dragged down with you."

Ethan leaned forward, his eyes locked onto Adrian's. "So, you're abandoning ship. You're choosing the easy way out."

Adrian's voice cracked, a hint of remorse in his tone. "I'm choosing survival, Ethan."

Ethan's lips curled into a bitter smile. "Survival? Is that what you call it? Abandoning your principles, your loyalty, and your duty to this company?"

Adrian's jaw tightened, his gaze hardening. "I've made my decision, Ethan. There's nothing more to discuss."

Ethan rose from his seat, his stance towering over Adrian. "Then go, Adrian. Leave. But know this—I won't forget this moment. I won't forget that when the chips were down, you chose to turn your back on me and this company."

Adrian stood, his resolve firm. "I'll take my chances, Ethan." With those parting words, Adrian turned and walked out of the office, leaving behind a heavy silence. Ethan watched him go, a mixture of anger and disappointment swirling within him. He had always considered Adrian a trusted ally, a friend even. Now that facade had shattered, and Ethan was left to face the battle ahead with one less ally by his side.

As the door closed behind Adrian, Ethan's office seemed to close in on him. He stood there, the weight of the confrontation settling on his shoulders. Anger, disappointment, and a lingering sense of betrayal churned within him, creating a storm of emotions he struggled to contain. He had always believed in the power of partnership, of standing together through thick and thin.

Yet, Adrian's decision to walk away from the company left a bitter taste in his mouth. The echoes of their heated exchange reverberated in his mind, the raw intensity of their words leaving wounds that cut deep.

He paced the room, his mind a whirlwind of thoughts. The weight of the responsibility he bore for the company's survival was now heavier than ever. Adrian's departure meant that he was left to face the storm alone. But amidst the anger and frustration, there was also a sense of grim determination. Ethan was no stranger to adversity; he had fought tooth and nail to build his empire from scratch. He had faced setbacks and challenges before. He wasn't about to let Adrian's departure derail him now.

As he stared out of the window, his jaw clenched, Ethan's gaze hardened. He was more resolved than ever to expose the truth, to root out the corruption that had infested his company. Adrian's departure might have wounded him, but it also ignited a fire within him—a relentless drive to prove that he was stronger than the challenges he faced.

Ethan's fingers clenched into fists, his knuckles

turning white with the force. He had thought that their bond was unbreakable. They were united in their fight against corruption and deceit. But now, a fracture had appeared, and the trust that once held them together had crumbled. Adrian's departure had changed the dynamics of their fight, but it hadn't changed Ethan's determination. If anything, it had only steeled his resolve to ensure that justice was served. Those who had betrayed him and his company would face the consequences.

The storm outside mirrored the storm within Ethan, but he was unyielding. With every step he took, he was moving closer to the truth. To the moment when the culprits would be exposed. To a point where his company's integrity would be restored. Adrian's departure had left a void, but it had also shown Ethan that he was more than capable of filling it—with his unwavering strength and resilience.

***

Ethan's steps were heavy as he made his way to

Isabella's office. His heart felt like a lead weight in his chest, burdened by the weight of the recent confrontation with Adrian. The office door seemed larger than usual, imposing and unyielding as he reached for the doorknob and let himself in.

Isabella looked up from her desk, her expression shifting from focused to concerned as she took in the sight of Ethan. His usually composed demeanor was shattered. His face was etched with lines of stress and fatigue. It was as if the weight of the world was resting on his shoulders, and he could no longer bear it alone.

"Ethan," Isabella said, rising from her seat. She could see the turmoil in his eyes, the pain that he was struggling to contain. She knew that something was wrong.

His voice wavered as he spoke, tinged with a vulnerability that he rarely allowed himself to show. "Isabella, I... I don't know where else to go. I just..." He trailed off, his throat tightening as he fought back the overwhelming rush of emotions.

Isabella crossed the room in swift strides, her concern deepening as she reached out to touch his arm. "Ethan, what happened? You can talk to me."

He took a shuddering breath, his gaze dropping to the floor as if unable to meet her eyes. "It's Adrian," he finally admitted, the words spilling out in a rush. "He... he confronted me today, Isabella. He said he's leaving the company, that he can't handle the pressure anymore."

Isabella's eyes widened, the news hitting her with unexpected force. She had known that tensions were running high, but she hadn't anticipated this drastic turn of events. She tightened her grip on his arm, offering him silent support as he continued. "He accused me of pushing him too far, of being blind to his struggles," Ethan's voice cracked. Isabella could hear the raw pain laced in his words. "And... he told me that he won't stand in the way of the investigation, but he's walking away."

Isabella's heart ached for Ethan as she watched

him unravel before her. She led him to a nearby chair and guided him to sit down. Taking a seat beside him, she offered a comforting presence, giving him the space he needed to let his emotions flow.

Ethan buried his face in his hands, his shoulders trembling as he let out a ragged sigh. "I trusted him, Isabella. Deep down, I hoped that he would come back to his senses. And now... now he's walking away."

Isabella placed a reassuring hand on his back, her touch a small gesture of solace. "Ethan, I'm so sorry. I know how much this means to you, and I can't imagine how betrayed you must feel right now."

He looked up at her, his eyes filled with a mixture of sadness and desperation. "Isabella, I don't know if I can do this on my own. The investigation, the company... it's all so overwhelming. And now with Adrian gone...he was my best friend."

Isabella's heart resonated with the raw pain in Ethan's voice. She understood the weight of his words, the sense of betrayal he must have been grappling with. As he buried his face in his hands, she felt a surge of empathy for him. She placed a hand on his back, offering a silent gesture of support.

"It's okay, Ethan," she whispered softly, her voice a soothing balm. "It's okay to feel hurt and disappointed. You're not alone in this anymore."

He looked up at her, his eyes reflecting a mix of frustration and vulnerability. "I know, Isabella, but it's just... He was more than a partner. He was like family. And now, it feels like he's turned his back on me."

Isabella nodded, her expression compassionate. "I can't imagine how hard this must be for you. But remember, we're a team too. And we're not going to let anything or anyone stand in our way."

Ethan's gaze met hers, and she saw a glimmer of determination amidst the pain. "You're right," he agreed, his voice steadier now. "We've come too far to let one person's betrayal define us. We have each other, and we have the truth on our side."

Isabella smiled, her touch lingering on his back. "Exactly. We're in this together, Ethan. And together, we're going to expose the fraud, no matter what it takes."

He managed a small, appreciative smile, the heaviness in his eyes starting to lift. "Thank you, Isabella. I don't know what I would do without you."

She squeezed his shoulder, her own resolve strengthening. "You'll never have to find out. We're a team, remember?"

Ethan's nod was filled with gratitude. Isabella knew that this moment was one of many they would face together. In that instant, Isabella realized that their partnership was evolving into something deeper. Something had transcended professional boundaries. They were becoming each other's pillars of strength. And as they leaned on each other, their shared determination to uncover the truth burned brighter than before.

***

Ethan's steps were heavy as he entered the grand living room of his mansion. His encounter with Adrian had left him drained. He was in no mood for any further complications. So, when James, his loyal butler, informed him that someone was waiting for him, he was puzzled. As he stepped into the room, his eyes settled on Amelia, seated on one of the plush couches. Her presence was unexpected, to say the least. It only added another layer of confusion to his already tumultuous day. He took a deep breath, summoning his composure, and walked towards her.

"Amelia," he greeted with a nod, his tone neutral.

"Ethan," she replied, her voice carrying a hint of warmth that seemed out of place.

"What brings you here?" he inquired, taking a seat across from her.

Amelia's eyes softened as she looked at him. "I've missed you, Ethan. It's been a while since we last saw each other."

He sighed. This was not what he needed right now. "Amelia, I've been dealing with a lot lately. I don't have the energy for..."

"I know," she interrupted, her expression pensive. "I've heard about the troubles with your company. It must be so stressful for you."

Ethan's brow furrowed. He appreciated her concern, but it felt misplaced, especially considering their history. "Amelia, I appreciate your concern, but I have things under control."

She leaned forward, her gaze intense. "Ethan, you don't have to face all this alone. I care about you, more than you realize. We had something special, and I can be a source of support for you."

He resisted the urge to roll his eyes. This was the

last thing he needed – Amelia trying to rekindle something that had long burned out. "Amelia, what we had is in the past. I've moved on, and I'm focused on different things now."

Her eyes flashed with a mix of frustration and hurt. "And what, or rather who, has captured your attention so much?"

Ethan's eyes bore into hers, his voice firm. "Isabella."

Amelia's reaction was immediate – a subtle tensing of her shoulders, a narrowing of her eyes. "Isabella, the detective? You've replaced me with her?"

Ethan's patience was wearing thin. "I haven't 'replaced' anyone, Amelia. Isabella is a colleague, a friend, and she's been a vital part of the recent developments in my life."

Amelia's facade crumbled, and her voice wavered. "But Ethan, you can't deny what we had. I love you."

His jaw tightened. He had had enough. "Amelia, what we had was nothing, it was a momentary lapse of judgement. And your attitude right now isn't helping your case. You need to respect my choices and my boundaries."

For a moment, Amelia's gaze held a mixture of defiance and vulnerability. Then, her demeanor shifted. She straightened her posture, her tone turning cold. "Fine, Ethan. If you've made your choice, then so be it. But don't expect me to stick around and watch you fall for some detective."

Ethan's frustration reached a breaking point. "You're right, Amelia. I won't expect that from you."

With that, he stood up, his tone final. "Goodbye, Amelia."

As he walked away, he couldn't help but feel a sense of relief mingled with exasperation. The encounter had drained him further. He knew he had made the right decision in asserting his boundaries.

Ethan's emotions were in turmoil as he navigated the aftermath of the intense day. The encounter with Amelia had left him emotionally drained. As he retreated to the quiet confines of his mansion, he couldn't help but replay the events of the day in his mind. The confrontation with Amelia stirred up emotions that he thought were long buried. He felt a mix of frustration and annoyance at her persistence in trying to rekindle a connection. It was clear to him that Amelia's intentions weren't genuine. It was obvious that she seemed more interested in possessing him than caring for him.

As he reflected on his reaction during the encounter, he felt a surge of pride. How he had stood his ground and asserted his boundaries was a testament to his growth and self-assuredness. Although it was a far cry from the man who had once been ensnared by Amelia's charms.

***

CHAPTER 13: THE FINAL SHOWDOWN

Their alliance was forged in fire. It was a partnership that had grown stronger with each obstacle they had overcome. Ethan's resources, coupled with Isabella's sharp intellect and skills, created a formidable team. As they joined forces, they knew that they had the power to bring down even the most cunning of fraudsters.

Days turned into nights as they pieced together the puzzle of corruption, and Isabella and Ethan grew closer. Their bond deepened with each shared victory and setback. They relied on each other for support, knowing that they were in this fight together.

The courtroom was filled with an air of tension. There was an invisible thread that seemed to pull at everyone's nerves. Isabella's gaze was fixed on the front, her heart pounding as she watched Ethan take the stand. He was confident, his shoulders squared as he prepared to present. They had the crucial piece of evidence that would expose the culprits behind the conspiracy.

Isabella's belief in Ethan was unshaken, her trust in him unwavering. She knew the truth he held. The determination that had driven him to uncover the depths of the corruption that had infiltrated his own company. Yet, as Ethan began to speak, his voice was strong and resolute. There was a sudden interruption that cut through the air like a knife.

A figure emerged from the shadows, striding purposefully toward the center of the courtroom. Isabella's heart sank as she recognized the man who had once been Ethan's partner – Adrian. He had betrayed Ethan before, and now he was poised to deliver another blow. Adrian's presence was like a dark cloud, casting a shadow over the proceedings.

Isabella's grip on her pen tightened, her knuckles turning white as she clenched her jaw. She exchanged a quick glance with Ethan, his expression a mixture of surprise and anger.

"Your Honor," Adrian began, his voice dripping with calculated disdain. "I must object to the evidence presented by the opposing side. It's clear that this is nothing more than a desperate attempt to salvage the reputation of my former partner."

The judge raised an eyebrow, a sense of curiosity evident in his expression. "On what grounds are you objecting, Mr. Wright?"

Adrian turned his gaze towards Ethan, a cold smile tugging at his lips. "Your Honor, I have evidence that Mr. Harrington has a history of being self-centered. He has a track record of putting his own interests above those of the company and his partners."

Isabella's heart hammered against her chest, her fingers trembling with suppressed anger. She knew Adrian was manipulating the situation.

She knew he was exploiting his past association with Ethan to cast doubt on the evidence at hand.

Ethan's jaw clenched, his fists balling at his sides. Isabella could practically feel the surge of emotions coursing through him – the anger, the frustration, the sheer disbelief at Adrian's audacity.

"Objection noted," the judge stated, his tone neutral. "Mr. Wright, you may proceed with your argument."

As Adrian launched into his diatribe, Isabella felt a surge of determination welling up inside her. She exchanged a quick glance with Ethan, their eyes locking in a silent understanding.

They couldn't let Adrian's manipulation stand. They had come too far and fought too hard to be undermined by his deceit. Ethan's voice cut through the air as he countered Adrian's accusations with poise.

Isabella marveled at his ability to maintain his composure in the face of such blatant attacks. She knew he was fighting not for his own reputation, but for the truth they had worked to uncover.

Ethan's eyes blazed with a fiery determination as he shot back. His voice was laced with controlled anger. "You're so quick to talk about history, Adrian. But let's not forget that it was your greed that tore this company apart in the first place. You sold out, betrayed not me but everyone who believed in us."

Adrian's lips curled into a mocking smile. "Ah, the noble crusader, always ready to play the victim. How predictable, Ethan."

Isabella's heart raced as she watched the exchange unfold. The tension in the air was palpable, and she could feel the weight of their animosity. It was a clash of wills, a battle between two men who had once been partners and now stood on opposite sides.

Ethan's jaw clenched, his fists tightening at his sides. "You were the one who chose to abandon ship when the going got tough. You left behind the company and the people who believed in us. And now you have the audacity to stand here and question my integrity?"

Adrian's laughter was cold and cutting. "Integrity? That's rich, coming from the man who's been digging up dirt on his own employees, who has been invading their privacy like some kind of authoritarian dictator."

Isabella could see Ethan's nostrils flare, his patience wearing thin. She knew how much he cared about his employees and how hard he had worked to root out corruption, aiming to ensure a fair and just workplace.

"That's not true, and you know it," Ethan's voice was steely. "I've been working to cleanse this company of the very poison you brought into it. I won't let you twist the truth to suit your own agenda."

Adrian's eyes glittered with a malicious glint. "Oh, spare me the hero act, Ethan. We both know you're trying to salvage your own image. You only want to play savior and distract everyone from your own failures."

Isabella felt the tension in the room escalate. The

air charged with their heated exchange. It was a clash of egos, a confrontation fueled by years of resentment and betrayal.

"You're the failure here, Adrian," Ethan's voice was a low, dangerous growl. "You're the one who let greed cloud your judgment, who sold out and left a trail of destruction behind you."

Adrian's face twisted with a mix of anger and disdain. "I made a smart business decision, Ethan. Something you were incapable of."

Isabella watched as Ethan's nostrils flared, his control slipping. She could sense the storm of emotions raging beneath his calm exterior, the pent-up anger and frustration that had been building for years.

"You call it a business decision, I call it a betrayal," Ethan's words were like a whip cracking through the air. "You left us all behind, and now you're back here, trying to undermine everything I've worked for."

Adrian's voice dripped with mockery. "Oh, spare me the wounded hero routine, Ethan. You're nothing more than a desperate man clinging to the last shreds of his empire."

Isabella could feel the intensity of the moment, the weight of their words hanging heavy in the air. It was a clash of ideals, a battle of egos. She knew that the outcome of this confrontation could have far-reaching consequences for both of them.

The judge's voice sliced through the heated exchange, his stern gaze fixed on Adrian. "Gentlemen, enough of this bickering. If you have evidence to support your claims, present it. Otherwise, we will not entertain baseless accusations."

Isabella's heart pounded in her chest as she watched, her anxiety mounting. She exchanged a quick glance with Ethan, her eyes reflecting the same frustration within him. They had worked hard to gather their evidence, to build a case against the fraudsters. But now it felt as if their efforts were being overshadowed by Adrian's theatrics.

Adrian's lips curled into a smug smile as he reached into a folder, pulling out a stack of documents. He handed them over to the court clerk, who passed them to the judge. Isabella's stomach churned as she realized the gravity of the situation. Adrian wasn't making baseless claims; he had physical proof to back up his accusations.

Ethan's jaw clenched, his knuckles turning white as he gripped the edge of the podium. Isabella could feel the waves of frustration rolling off him, his anger simmering beneath the surface. She wanted to reach out, to offer some form of comfort, but they were both trapped in this tense courtroom drama.

The judge's eyes scanned the documents. His expression grew more serious with each passing moment. Isabella's heart sank as she saw the judge's brows furrow, his lips thinning into a tight line. It was clear that Adrian's evidence had struck a chord, casting a shadow of doubt over their case.

"Very well," the judge finally spoke, his voice measured. "These documents warrant further investigation. We will adjourn for the day and reconvene once we have examined the evidence presented."

Isabella's shoulders slumped as a sense of defeat washed over her. She exchanged a helpless look with Ethan, their frustration mirroring each other's. It was a setback, a blow to their constructed case. And worst of all, Adrian's tactics had managed to cast doubt on their credibility.

As the court began to disperse, Isabella felt a heavy weight settle in her chest. She had seen firsthand the lengths to which their enemies were willing to go to undermine their efforts. The anxiety that had been building within her now threatened to overwhelm her.

Ethan's jaw remained clenched as he turned to Isabella. His eyes burned with a mixture of determination and anger. "We can't let this setback deter us, Isabella. We'll regroup, reevaluate our evidence, and come back stronger."

Isabella nodded, her resolve unwavering despite the turmoil that churned within her. She knew that they couldn't afford to back down now, not when they were so close to exposing the truth.

"You're right," she replied, her voice steady. "We've come too far to let this setback define us. We'll use this time to strengthen our case. To ensure that when we return to that courtroom, we have the evidence needed to prove our claims."

Ethan's lips quirked into a determined smile. There was a flicker of hope cutting through the frustration. "We'll show them that we won't be swayed by empty accusations. We'll come back stronger than ever."

As they left the courtroom, Isabella couldn't shake the feeling of unease that lingered in the air. The battle was far from over. The road ahead was fraught with challenges and uncertainties. But she was determined to stand by Ethan's side, to weather the storm together.

***

Isabella and Ethan sat across from each other in a softly lit corner of a quiet café. Their minds raced with thoughts of their next move. The setback in the courtroom had cast a shadow over their plans, leaving them with a sense of urgency to regroup and strengthen their case.

"I can't believe how close we were," Ethan muttered, his frustration palpable. "If we had just been able to present that evidence without any interruptions..."

Isabella nodded in agreement, her brows furrowing in thought. "I know. But we can't let this discourage us. We have other pieces of evidence that can still expose their fraudulent activities."

As they were discussing their options, Isabella's phone vibrated on the table. It drew her attention. She picked it up and saw a text message from Jane, the employee who had become her confidant within the company. Her heart quickened as she opened the message and saw a series of photos and audio files attached.

"What is it?" Ethan asked, noticing the change in Isabella's expression.

Isabella's eyes widened as she scrolled through the photos and audio files. "It's from Jane. She's sending us evidence from the warehouse where they've been conducting illegal activities. And there are audio recordings of Mr. Benson confessing to her about the secret alliance."

Ethan leaned forward, his eyes focused on the screen of Isabella's phone. "This could be a game-changer. Let me see."

Isabella handed him the phone, and he began to examine the photos and listen to the audio recordings. As he did, his expression shifted from surprise to determination.

"This is it," he said, his voice low but resolute. "This is the evidence we need to expose them."

Isabella nodded, her heart pounding with a renewed sense of purpose. "With this, we can finally reveal their true intentions and the extent of their fraud."

Ethan handed the phone back to Isabella, his gaze unwavering. "We need to make sure this evidence is secure and that it can't be tampered with. We can't afford any more setbacks."

Isabella nodded in agreement. "I'll make copies and store them in a safe location. And I'll let Jane know that we've received the evidence."

As Isabella began to type a response to Jane's message, Ethan's phone buzzed on the table. He picked it up and saw a message from his lawyer, updating him on the latest developments of the court case.

"More legal hurdles," Ethan muttered, his frustration evident. Isabella looked up from her phone, her determination unwavering. "We can't let that deter us. We have the evidence now, and we'll use it to our advantage."

Ethan met her gaze, a mixture of gratitude and determination in his eyes. "Thank you, Isabella. Your dedication and relentless pursuit of the truth... it's given me hope in the midst of all this chaos."

As they left the café, their minds were focused on the path ahead. With the newfound evidence in their possession, they felt a renewed sense of purpose. The road might still be fraught with challenges, but they were more determined than ever to expose the fraudsters.

Isabella smiled, a sense of camaraderie and trust blossoming between them. "We're in this together,

Ethan. We'll see it through, no matter what."

***

CHAPTER 14: LOVE'S TRIUMPH OVER DARKNESS

The courtroom buzzed with anticipation as Isabella and Ethan stood side by side. Their lawyer was ready to present the final blow against the fraudulent schemes. Their legal team had worked hard to prepare the evidence that Jane had provided. They were about to reveal the extent of the corruption that had taken place within the company.

Ethan's lawyer stood before the judge. There was a confident and determined expression on his face. He held up a stack of documents and began to present the evidence, detailing the illegal activities that had been uncovered through the photos and audio recordings.

As he spoke, the courtroom fell silent, the weight of the accusations hanging in the air. Adrian, seated at the opposing table, appeared unsettled. His usual air of confidence had waned, now replaced by a growing unease as the evidence against him mounted. Isabella watched his reaction, a sense of satisfaction blooming within her.

The judge listened as the evidence was presented. Isabella could sense the shifting dynamics in the room. People exchanged uneasy glances, and whispers of disbelief spread through the crowd. It was becoming clear that the accusations against Adrian held merit. His once-impeccable reputation was unraveling.

Ethan leaned closer to Isabella, his voice a low, confident whisper. "We're getting closer, Isabella. We're exposing the truth."

Isabella nodded, her heart pounding with a mixture of excitement and nervous anticipation. As the evidence continued to unfold, it became evident that the fraudulent activities extended beyond Adrian. The web of corruption was being untangled, piece by piece, in front of the court's watchful eyes.

Finally, as the evidence was presented in its entirety, Ethan's lawyer stepped back. His gaze was fixed on Adrian. "Your Honor, it is clear that the opposing party has engaged in a series of illegal activities. These have not only damaged my client's company but also deceived the public and shareholders. We ask for a thorough investigation into these matters and appropriate legal action against those involved."

The judge's stern expression revealed his understanding of the gravity of the situation. He turned his attention to Adrian, who appeared to be struggling to maintain his composure.

"Mr. Adrian," the judge began, his voice firm, "You are hereby ordered to cooperate with any investigations into the allegations against you. This court will not tolerate such blatant disregard for the law and the trust of the public."

As the verdict was delivered, a sense of vindication washed over Isabella. The truth had prevailed, and justice was being served. She glanced at Ethan, whose face was a mix of relief and satisfaction. She couldn't help but feel a surge of pride for what they had accomplished together.

Outside the courtroom, Jane stood nervously, awaiting Isabella and Ethan's exit. When they finally emerged, their faces beamed with triumph and gratitude. Isabella approached Jane, her eyes shimmering with emotion.

"Jane," Isabella said, her voice filled with gratitude, "you have no idea how much your bravery and honesty have meant to us. You've helped us uncover the truth and bring those responsible to justice."

Jane smiled, her eyes shining with a mixture of pride and relief. "I was doing what was right. I couldn't stand by and watch them get away with it."

Isabella replied with a warm smile, her eyes reflecting gratitude and curiosity. "Jane, I can't thank you enough for what you've done. You've been a lifesaver in this whole situation."

Jane returned the smile, though a hint of sheepishness colored her expression. "I'm glad I could finally come forward and help. I'm sorry it took me so long, Isabella."

Isabella's brow furrowed in gentle confusion. "I understand you were scared, Jane, but I can't help wondering… What kept you from reaching out to me sooner?"

Her eyes dropped to the ground for a moment, her fingers twisting. "It's that… Mr. Benson,… he warned me not to say anything. He made it clear that if I spoke up, there would be consequences. I was scared for my safety, Isabella."

Isabella's empathy deepened as she listened. She realized the gravity of the situation Jane had been facing. "I'm so sorry you had to go through that, Jane. But why now? What changed?"

Jane's gaze lifted to meet Isabella's, determination now replacing the apprehension. "When I saw the news about Mr. Benson's arrest and the court hearings, I knew that things were finally changing. It gave me hope that justice might actually prevail. And I couldn't let your hard work and Mr. Ethan's dedication go to waste. You both deserved to know the truth."

Isabella nodded, her admiration for Jane growing with each word. "Thank you for having the courage to come forward. Especially after everything you've been through."

Jane's smile regained its strength. "I couldn't have done it without the support of people like you and Mr. Ethan. You showed me that standing up for the truth is worth the risk."

Isabella's hand gently touched Jane's arm. "You're very brave, Jane. Your courage is going to make a difference, not just for us but for everyone affected by this."

Jane's eyes shimmered with gratitude as she nodded. "I hope so. And thank you for believing in me."

As they shared a heartfelt moment, Isabella couldn't help but reflect on the power of solidarity. The resilience of those who dared to stand up against corruption. Jane's determination was a testament to the strength of the human spirit. Isabella was more committed than ever to ensuring that the truth prevailed. With Jane's evidence, they were well on their way to dismantling the fraudulent web.

As Isabella waited outside, Ethan came out with a huge grin on his face. Not only had he won against the fraudsters, but he had also regained his public trust and reputation. Walking toward her, Ethan's lips curved into a genuine smile, his eyes reflecting a myriad of emotions. "Isabella, we did it."

Her smile mirrored his, a shared moment of triumph passing between them. "Yes, Ethan, we did. The truth prevailed."

As the reality of their victory settled in, Ethan felt an immense sense of pride. It was not only for himself but for the entire team that had rallied behind them. Their collective efforts had exposed the corruption that had threatened his company. It was a victory for integrity, for standing up against those who sought to exploit and manipulate.

But beneath the pride and satisfaction, there was also a deep sense of humility. Ethan realized that he couldn't have done it alone. Isabella had been his partner, his confidante, and his anchor throughout this ordeal. Her belief in him, even in the face of adversity, had been a driving force. He hadn't realized she was pushing him to push back against the darkness.

As they stood outside the court, finally letting out a sigh of relief, Ethan turned to Isabella, his eyes reflecting the gratitude and respect he felt. "Isabella, thank you. Thank you for everything."

She met his gaze, her own eyes shimmering with emotion. "Ethan, it was an honor to stand by your side.

We faced the storm together, and we came out stronger because of it."

***

Ethan sat in his office, a sense of gratitude and relief washing over him. He picked up his phone and dialed Jane's number. He was eager to express his appreciation for her role in their recent victory. After a few rings, she answered, her voice filled with a mixture of exhaustion and triumph.

"Jane, it's Ethan," he began, his tone sincere and warm. "I wanted to thank you for what you've done. Your bravery and determination were instrumental in helping us uncover the truth and turn the tide in our favor."

There was a brief pause on the other end, followed by Jane's heartfelt response. "Mr. Harrington, I couldn't stand by and watch the company I have dedicated years to be tarnished by those schemers. It was the right thing to do."

Ethan smiled, his admiration evident in his voice. "Your actions went above and beyond, Jane. You've not only saved our company, but you've also shown immense integrity. I'm grateful for your loyalty and courage."

Jane's voice carried a mix of pride and humility. "Thank you, Mr. Harrington. I believe in the company's mission. I couldn't let it be dismantled by dishonest individuals."

Ethan nodded, even though Jane couldn't see him. "Your dedication and the evidence you provided were crucial in exposing the culprits. We couldn't have done it without you."

"I'm glad I could help," Jane replied. "The truth needed to be revealed, and I'm relieved we were able to set things right."

Ethan's tone was firm and appreciative. "Rest assured, your efforts won't go unnoticed. We'll make sure you're recognized for your contribution."

Jane's gratitude was evident as she spoke. "Thank you, Mr. Harrington. It's been a tough journey, but seeing justice prevail is its own reward."

Ethan concluded the conversation with genuine warmth. "I wanted to discuss something with you. Can you come to my office?"

"Of course, I'll be right there," Jane replied.

A short while later, there was a knock on his office door. Jane entered, her expression a mix of curiosity and anticipation. "You wanted to see me, Mr. Harrington?"

Ethan gestured for her to take a seat. "Please, have a seat, Jane." As she settled into the chair, Ethan leaned forward, his hands clasped on his desk.

"Jane, I wanted to express my deepest gratitude for your efforts during these times. Your courage and commitment played a pivotal role. You have immensely helped in uncovering the truth and ensuring justice prevailed."

Jane nodded, her professionalism giving way to a hint of humility. "Thank you, Mr. Harrington. I believe it was the right thing to do."

Ethan smiled, his eyes fixed on her. "And because of that, you deserve a new opportunity. Jane, effective immediately, I would like to offer you the position of Director in place of Mr. Benson."

Jane's eyes widened, her surprise evident. "Director? But Mr. Harrington, I..." Ethan raised a hand to interrupt her. "Jane, your dedication, integrity, and leadership qualities have not gone unnoticed. You've proven that you have what it takes to lead with excellence."

Jane's voice wavered as she responded, her emotions getting the better of her. "I'm honored, Mr. Harrington. This means a lot to me."

Ethan leaned back in his chair, a genuine smile

playing on his lips. "You've earned it, Jane. Your promotion is well-deserved, and I have full confidence in your ability to excel in this new role."

Jane's gratitude was palpable as she nodded. "I won't let you down, Mr. Harrington. I'll give my best to lead the company with honesty and dedication."

"I have no doubt about that," Ethan replied. "Your appointment as Director is a testament to our commitment to transparency. I hope you won't forget the integrity and the values we stand for."

As they discussed the details of her new role, Jane's excitement grew. Ethan had not only given her a promotion but had also entrusted her with significant responsibility. It was a symbol of how the company had evolved, learning from its past mistakes and embracing a brighter future.

Ethan's decision to promote Jane was a reflection of his belief in the power of those who stood up for what was right. As he watched her leave his office, he couldn't help but feel a sense of pride and optimism. With Jane at the helm, he knew that the company was in capable hands, ready to face the challenges that lay ahead and continue their journey toward a more ethical future.

***

The night sky was adorned with a blanket of stars, each one casting a shimmering reflection upon the dark waves below. A gentle sea breeze rustled through the air, carrying with it a hint of salt and adventure. On this splendid evening, Ethan's grand vision came to life upon the expansive deck of a luxurious cruise ship.

The opulent vessel was beautifully decorated with cascading curtains of rich fabrics in shades of deep blue and gold, creating an ambiance of regal sophistication. Crystal chandeliers dangled from above, casting a soft, warm glow. The deck was a tapestry of extravagance, adorned with lush flower arrangements, comfortable seating, and artful displays of gourmet delights.

Ethan himself stood at the center of it all, his presence exuding a blend of confidence and charm. He was dressed in a tailored tuxedo of deep navy, the intricate patterns woven into the fabric shimmering under the ambient lighting. The crispness of his attire spoke of meticulous attention to detail, the cut of his ensemble accentuating his commanding presence.

As he gazed out over the sea, a sense of accomplishment washed over him. The cruise party was a celebration not only of the success of his company, but of the journey he had undertaken alongside Isabella. It was a testament to their unyielding dedication and their determination to root out corruption. Ethan's smile was genuine as he mingled with the guests, engaging in lively conversations that ranged from business matters to light-hearted banter. He was the consummate host, ensuring that each attendee felt welcome and appreciated. But beneath his polished exterior, his mind couldn't help but drift to Isabella.

"Ethan, you've outdone yourself with this party.

Everything is exquisite," said the director of one of the stakeholder communities.

"Thank you, I'm delighted you're enjoying it. Our team worked hard to make sure it was a memorable evening for everyone," Ethan said humbly.

"And it is. You're quite the host, mingling with everyone, making sure we all feel welcome. You were one of the very first companies that stood in solidarity after the court declared us clear."

"Well, it's important to me that everyone has a good time. Plus, I enjoy these conversations, whether they're about business or simply enjoying the night," Ethan replied, chuckling. But in actuality, his mind was somewhere else. He was waiting for Isabella. After the victory of bringing down their enemies, their relationship had grown immensely. His eyes scanned the crowd, seeking her out amidst the sea of dressed-up guests.

When his gaze finally landed on her, his heart

skipped a beat. Isabella was a vision in a flowing gown of midnight blue, the hue accentuating her captivating features. The dress itself was a work of art, with beadwork and delicate lace adding a touch of ethereal beauty to her already striking presence. Ethan was in awe, realizing just how ethereal she could look, truly mesmerized.

The moonlight painted a shimmering path on the water as Ethan and Isabella stood on the top deck of the luxurious yacht. Soft music played in the background, mingling with the gentle lapping of the waves. He offered his arm to her, a mischievous glint in his eyes.

The moonlit sky cast a soft, ethereal glow over the yacht as it rocked on the tranquil waters. Ethan and Isabella stood at the edge of the deck. The soft breeze ruffled their hair as they gazed out at the shimmering expanse before them.

The sound of the lapping waves and the distant hum of the city created a serene symphony around them.

Isabella turned towards Ethan. Her eyes met his with an intensity that mirrored the depth of their connection. Time seemed to stand still as they locked eyes. There was a silent understanding passing between them. Ethan's hand found its way to Isabella's cheek, his touch gentle and reverent.

"I can't believe we made it through all that," Ethan murmured, his voice laced with emotion. "Together." Isabella's lips curled into a soft smile. "It wasn't an easy journey, but it was worth it."

Ethan's thumb brushed across Isabella's cheek. His touch sent a shiver of anticipation down her spine. He leaned in, his lips hovering inches from hers. Isabella's heart raced, the world around them narrowing to the two of them at that moment.

Their lips met in a tender, hesitant kiss. It was a sweet exploration, a gentle intertwining of souls that spoke of the shared trials. Isabella's fingers found their way to Ethan's chest. She could feel the steady beat of his heart beneath her touch, a comforting reassurance.

As the kiss deepened, the spark between them ignited into a passionate flame. Ethan's arms wrapped around Isabella, pulling her closer as their bodies pressed together. Isabella's fingers tangled in his hair. It was a kiss that spoke of their journey, their shared experiences, and their unwavering bond. It was a promise of a future filled with love, trust, and a lifetime of adventures together. The world around them faded away, leaving only the warmth of their connection and the intoxicating taste of each other's lips.

Finally, they pulled away, their breaths mingling in the cool night air. Ethan rested his forehead against Isabella's, his eyes closed as he savored the moment. "Isabella, I want you to know that you've changed my life in ways I never thought possible."

Isabella's heart swelled with emotion, her eyes glistening with unshed tears. "And you've shown me a world of strength, resilience, and love that I never knew existed."

Their foreheads remained pressed together as their souls intertwined in a moment of pure connection. The yacht sailed on, carrying them through the starlit night. But their love bloomed under the moon's watchful gaze. And as the night enveloped them, their hearts beat as one, forever entwined in a love that had weathered storms and emerged stronger on the other side.

***

"Shall we, Detective? Our private retreat awaits," he said, a playful smirk playing on his face.

"I must admit, Mr. Harrington, your ability to surprise me is becoming quite a skill," she said, raising an eyebrow at him.

"A necessary talent, I assure you. Now, our destination awaits," Ethan replied, chuckling. He led her through a dimly lit corridor, and as they reached the entrance to the private floor, Ethan held open the door with a flourish.

"After you," he smiled, nodding for her to go on.

"Impressive. You went all out, didn't you?" Isabella glanced around as the warm glow of moonlight and candles escalated the surroundings.

"Only the best for my esteemed partner," Ethan replied, smiling.

The room was adorned with twinkling fairy lights, casting a warm and inviting glow. A table was set for two, adorned with elegant dinnerware and a centerpiece of roses. The gentle sway of the yacht added an extra layer of intimacy to the ambiance.

"Are you trying to sweep me off my feet, Ethan?" she asked, teasing him.

"Is it working?" Ethan leaned in and murmured to her.

"Perhaps. But I won't be easy to win over, you know," she said, matching his tone.

"Challenge accepted," Ethan smirked.

They took their seats. The soft strains of the music created an enchanting backdrop for their conversation.

"So, is this where you confess that all those extravagant gestures were part of an elaborate plan to distract me from your true intentions?" Isabella asked him playfully.

"Whatever do you mean, Detective? I'm a man who appreciates fine company and good food," Ethan replied, mocking her.

"Right, because planning an entire candlelit dinner on a yacht is what every man does on a whim," Isabella said, raising an eyebrow at him.

"Well, you know what they say, Detective. Go big or go home," he said as he leaned back in his chair, smirking.

"I can't argue with that logic," Isabella rolled her eyes at his response.

Their banter continued as the courses were served. Each dish was a delight for the senses. The conversation flowed, ranging from their past experiences to their hopes for the future. There was a camaraderie between them.

"You know, Ethan, for a man who's surrounded by power plays, you have a surprising knack for creating romantic settings," she said, smirking as they were served their last meal, the dessert of the night. Isabella already felt full because of nervousness.

"Are you implying that I'm all business, Miss Isabella?" he asked her, questioning her.

"Well, it wouldn't be the first time you've surprised me," Isabella leaned in closer to him, her tone suggestive.

"Is that a challenge, Detective?" Ethan smirked. At first, Isabella paused and locked her gaze into Ethan's.

"Perhaps it is," she said finally.

Their eyes held a charged intensity, the unspoken tension between them palpable. At that moment, the world seemed to fade away, leaving only the two of them in their own private universe.

"You intrigue me, Isabella. More than I thought possible," Ethan said finally, giving in.

"And you, Mr. Harrington. You have managed to capture my curiosity in ways I never expected," Isabella said, matching his tone.

As they finally stood up from the table, Ethan offered his hand to Isabella.

"Must we dance?" Ethan said, smiling.

"Lead the way, Ethan," Isabella said, holding his hand. They swayed to the music, their bodies moving in perfect harmony. The stars above and the gentle lull of the waves below seemed to mirror the rhythm of their hearts.

"Isabella, I may be a man of power and influence, but there's one thing I've learned throughout all this," Ethan leaned into her and whispered into her ear. His warm breath on her ear sent shudders down her spine.

"And what's that?" Isabella asked, curiosity brimming through her eyes.

"That the most valuable asset one can own is trust. And I want you to know, Isabella Knight, that you have mine – completely," he said, smiling softly. The pale moonlight was making his appearance more magical than it already was.

"And you have mine," Isabella said as she felt flutters in her chest.

"I love you, Isabella," he confessed, whispering.

"And I love you, Ethan," replied Isabella, feeling like she has everything she ever wanted. They embraced, their hearts beating in perfect sync. At that moment, amidst the grandeur of the yacht, their connection felt unbreakable. They had faced challenges, uncovered secrets, and navigated treacherous waters together. Their love was a testament to the trials they had overcome and the unbreakable bond they had formed.

***

In the days that followed, the truth came to light like a cleansing tide. It swept away the fraudulent schemes and deceit that had plagued Ethan's company. The evidence they gathered exposed the culprits for who they were. Mr. Benson's web of lies unraveled, and he faced the consequences of his actions. His empire of deception crumbled around him. Adrian's true intentions were exposed to the public, tarnishing his reputation beyond repair. The veil of charm and charisma that he had worn shattered, revealing a man driven by greed and a thirst for power. His partnership with the other fraudsters was laid bare.

Mr. Wilson, once a mentor figure to Isabella, was held accountable for his role in the conspiracy. The revelation of his betrayal sent shockwaves through the business community. His influence waned as the truth emerged. Ethan's company, though battered by the storm of accusations, emerged stronger than ever. The public rallied behind him, recognizing his determination to uphold honesty and integrity. With Isabella by his side, they constructed a comprehensive restructuring that would ensure the company's future success.

As the dust settled, Isabella stood on the rooftop of a building, looking out over the city. The sun dipped below the horizon, casting a warm glow that reflected the sense of accomplishment she felt. She had come a long way from the detective who had embarked on this journey. She knew that her partnership with Ethan had forever changed her.

Ethan joined her on the rooftop, his presence a reassuring anchor.

"It's finally over, Isabella. The storm has passed, and we've weathered it together," Ethan said softly.

"Yes. It's hard to believe that everything we've been through has led us here," Isabella replied, nodding slightly.

"And here is exactly where I want to be. Isabella, there's something I've been wanting to ask you," he replied, smiling. Isabella's heart skipped a beat as she turned to face him, her eyes locking with his.

"What is it, Ethan?" She asked, curious about his intentions.

Taking a deep breath, Ethan started, "Isabella, from the moment we met, you've been my partner, my confidante, and my rock. You've shown me what true strength and unwavering dedication look like. And amidst all the chaos and danger, you've become something even more to me." Isabella's breath caught in her throat as Ethan dropped to one knee, his hand reaching into his pocket.

She could feel the vulnerability-soaked words. Her heart skipped a beat as she took the box from him, her gaze fixed on the contents. She opened it, revealing a stunning diamond ring that sparkled even in the setting sun.

"Isabella, will you marry me? Will you be my partner, my confidante, and my ally for all the days to come?" He said finally, his voice full of sincere emotions.

Isabella's breath caught in her throat as she looked up from the ring, her eyes meeting Ethan's. The weight of the moment hung in the air. The promise of a future together that neither of them could have predicted.

"But... what about…" she asked hesitantly.

"There has been no one but you, my dear Isabella.

No one but you rules my heart," he explained as a cold breeze ran through them. The soft music in the background added to the romantic aura in the surroundings. Isabella had not realized that someone she had met would turn out to be the love of her life.

"Ethan... I've always believed in seeking the truth, no matter how challenging or daunting the path may be. And in this journey with you, I've found not only a worthy cause but a kindred spirit," Isabella replied, smiling warmly.

"Isabella..." Ethan's anxiety was rushing; he could feel his heart pounding in his chest.

"Yes, Ethan. Yes, I will marry you." Tears rolled down her cheeks as she smiled, glowing from the inside out. Ethan's face broke into a radiant smile, his eyes shining with happiness. He took the ring from the box and slid it onto Isabella's finger. The diamond gleamed. It was a symbol of their shared commitment and the bond they had forged through adversity.

"You've made me the happiest man, Isabella," Ethan said, smiling softly.

"And you've given me a future I never imagined." Isabella felt like her whole life had changed over the course of a few months.

***

Months passed, and their engagement was celebrated by their friends, families, and colleagues. Plans for their wedding were crafted, a harmonious blend of their respective worlds. The grand event was a reflection of their journey. It was a fusion of opulence and modesty, both symbolizing their shared values and the unity they had achieved.

They shared a quiet moment, gazing at the city that had been the backdrop to their fight for justice. Their journey had been marked by obstacles and danger, but it had also been one of growth, trust, and an unexpected love that had blossomed amidst the chaos. Only with the power of true love were they able to overcome the many impossible obstacles.

As Isabella and Ethan's love story continued to unfold, they found themselves embarking on a new journey together: the journey towards their wedding day. The planning process was a delightful mix of excitement and a touch of chaos.

They both worked together to create a celebration that would mark the beginning of their forever. The first step was selecting the perfect venue after careful consideration. They settled on a picturesque countryside estate surrounded by rolling hills, blooming gardens, and a charming vintage mansion. It was a setting that captured the timeless romance they shared.

Isabella immersed herself in the wedding planning, poring over every detail. She chose a color palette of soft blush, ivory, and gold, reflecting both elegance and intimacy. The invitations were a work of art, featuring delicate calligraphy and a subtle hint of the moon and stars to symbolize their deep connection.

Ethan, ever the attentive groom-to-be, was involved every step of the way. He focused on ensuring that the entertainment and menu were exquisite. The couple's shared love for music was evident in the live band they selected, promising to keep the dance floor alive all night.

One of the most memorable moments of the planning process was the selection of Isabella's wedding gown. Surrounded by her closest friends and family, she tried on dresses that ranged from classic to modern. The moment she stepped into a gown that was both elegant and breathtaking, she knew it was the one. She knew that it would light up Ethan's eyes when he saw her walking down the aisle.

Within weeks to go before the big day, Isabella and Ethan were faced with a sudden decision. They had always envisioned an intimate gathering, surrounded by their closest loved ones. Yet, as the RSVPs poured in, they found that the guest list had grown larger than they had anticipated. A difficult choice lay ahead of them: either they were to stick to their original vision or adjust their plans to accommodate the unexpected turnout. After much heartfelt conversation, Isabella and Ethan made the decision to welcome all those who wanted to celebrate with them. They realized that their love was meant to be shared, and the more, the merrier. It was a beautiful testament to their generous spirits and their ability to adapt.

***

The sun was setting, casting a warm golden glow over the tranquil surroundings. Isabella and Ethan found themselves standing at the edge of a serene lake. Their reflections danced upon the water's surface, mirroring the excitement that pulsed through their hearts.

Isabella fiddled with the delicate necklace around her neck, a nervous habit she had developed over the years. She stole a glance at Ethan, who seemed lost in his own thoughts. A gentle breeze rustled the leaves, carrying with it a sense of calmness that they both needed.

Ethan turned to Isabella, his gaze soft yet intense. "You know, I never thought I'd be the nervous type," he admitted with a wistful smile. Isabella chuckled, her musical sound easing the tension for Ethan. "Well, I think it's safe to say that weddings tend to do that to people, even billionaires."

He reached out to tuck a loose strand of hair behind her ear, his touch sending a shiver down her spine. "I guess you're right. But you, Isabella, have a way of making even the most nerve-wracking moments feel like an adventure."

She met his gaze, her eyes shining with a mixture of emotions. "And you, Ethan, have a knack for turning ordinary moments into something extraordinary."

The air was charged with unspoken words, the

depth of their connection palpable. Ethan took Isabella's hands in his, his touch warm and reassuring. "You know, as much as I wish we could fast forward to our wedding day, I also want to savor every moment leading up to it."

Isabella nodded, a soft smile gracing her lips. "Me too. It's like the final chapter of our journey is about to begin."

He leaned in, his forehead resting against hers. "And what a journey it's been. From solving mysteries to facing adversaries, we've seen it all. But through it all, one thing has remained constant – our love."

Isabella closed her eyes, allowing his words to wash over her. "I couldn't agree more. Our love has been the anchor, the steady force that's guided us through every storm."

Ethan pulled her into a gentle embrace. Their bodies fitted together as if they were two puzzle pieces finding their perfect match. "Well, you know what they say. You can know when it's your person. I promise you, Isabella, that no matter what challenges come our way, I'll always be by your side."

She rested her head against his chest, feeling the steady rhythm of his heartbeat. "And I promise to stand beside you, to support you, and to love you through every twist and turn."

As they stood there, wrapped in each other's arms, the nerves seemed to dissipate, leaving behind a sense of serenity and contentment. The setting sun cast a warm embrace around them, a reflection of the love that illuminated their hearts. "Isabella," Ethan whispered, his voice a tender caress. "I can't wait to see you walking down the aisle, to make you my wife."

A soft blush-tinged Isabella's cheeks as she looked up at him. Her eyes shone with unshed tears of happiness. "And I can't wait to say 'I do' and become your wife."

Their lips met in a sweet, lingering kiss, sealing

their promises to one another. At that moment, as the sun dipped below the horizon and the world seemed to stand still, Isabella and Ethan knew that their love was unbreakable. Their wedding day would mark the beginning of a new chapter filled with love and endless possibilities.

***

Their wedding day was a spectacular affair, a blend of sophistication and intimacy that encapsulated their journey. The venue, a sprawling estate nestled amidst lush gardens, was adorned with elegant decorations. Soft hues of gold, blush, and ivory dominated the color palette, exuding an air of timeless romance. As the sun began to set, casting a golden glow over the surroundings, guests started to gather in anticipation of the ceremony.

Isabella's bridal party, dressed in flowing gowns that complemented the color scheme, exuded an aura of joy as they helped her prepare for the momentous occasion. Her gown, a stunning creation of delicate lace and beadwork, captured her beauty and grace. Meanwhile, Ethan and his groomsmen exuded charm in tailored tuxedos, their smiles reflecting the excitement of the day. The atmosphere was filled with a sense of celebration.

As the ceremony began, an air of anticipation filled the space. The aisle was lined with fragrant blossoms, and a gentle breeze carried the sweet melody of a string quartet. Isabella made her grand entrance, her radiant smile illuminated by the setting sun. Ethan's eyes never left her as she walked towards him, her steps steady yet filled with emotion.

In the soft, glowing light of the bridal suite, Isabella stood before a full-length mirror. Her reflection was adorned in a breathtaking wedding gown. Her heart raced with a mix of excitement and nerves as she smoothed a stray strand of hair behind her ear. Jane, her loyal friend and confidante, stood by her side, a warm smile on her face.

"Isabella, you look stunning," Jane said, her voice

filled with genuine admiration.

Isabella offered a grateful smile. Her fingers traced the delicate lace that adorned her gown. "Thank you, Jane. I still can't believe this day is finally here."

Jane chuckled softly, her eyes sparkling with affection. "I remember when we first met during work together. I never would've imagined that we'd end up here, preparing for your wedding."

Isabella's gaze met Jane's in the mirror, and a soft chuckle escaped her lips. "Life has a way of surprising us, doesn't it?"

Jane nodded, her smile turning sentimental. "It does. And I have to say, seeing you and Ethan together, it's like a fairy tale come true."

Isabella's eyes shimmered with emotion as she thought about Ethan. "He's been my rock through all the challenges we've faced. I can't imagine my life without him."

Jane's expression grew more tender. "And he can't imagine his life without you, either. I've seen the way he looks at you, Isabella. It's a look of unwavering love and devotion."

A soft sigh escaped Isabella as she took in Jane's words. "I feel the same way about him, Jane. But I have to admit, I'm feeling a bit overwhelmed right now. Walking down that aisle, facing all those eyes… it's a lot to take in."

Jane stepped closer and gently placed a hand on Isabella's shoulder. "You don't have to do it alone, you know. We're all here for you, supporting you every step of the way."

Isabella's gaze met Jane's once more, her heart swelling with gratitude. "I'm so lucky to have you in my life, Jane. Your friendship has meant the world to me."

Jane's smile was soft and reassuring. "And you've meant as much to me. We've been through so much together, Isabella. I have no doubt that you'll handle this moment with the same grace and strength you've always shown."

Tears welled up in Isabella's eyes as she nodded, her emotions threatening to spill over. "Thank you, Jane."

Jane pulled her into a warm embrace, holding her tightly. "You've got this, Isabella. And remember, Ethan is waiting for you at the end of that aisle. As long as you two are together, there's nothing you can't overcome."

Isabella clung to the embrace, finding solace and comfort in Jane's words. As they pulled apart, a sense of calm settled over her. "You're right. I'm ready."

Jane gave her a reassuring pat on the arm. "That's the spirit. Now, let's get you down that aisle and into the arms of the man who loves you more than anything."

With a final shared smile, Isabella took a deep

breath and nodded. With Jane by her side, she felt a renewed sense of confidence and determination. As they left the bridal suite and made their way toward the ceremony, Isabella knew that she was not only embarking on a new chapter of her life but doing so surrounded by love and support.

***

On their special day, Isabella and Ethan stood on the precipice of a new chapter in their lives. They couldn't help but feel the absence of their beloved parents. The ache of missing them was particularly poignant on this day, meant for celebrating love and unity.

Ethan's thoughts often drifted to his mother. She was a graceful and kind-hearted woman whose memory was etched in his heart. He wished she could have been there to witness his union with Isabella. The void left by her absence was a reminder of the unconditional love she had given him. He carried her teachings with him, knowing that she would have embraced Isabella.

And under the warm embrace of the sun and surrounded by their loved ones, Ethan and Isabella stood before each other, ready to exchange their vows.

Isabella's heart raced as she looked into Ethan's eyes. Her voice quivered with emotion. "Ethan, from the moment we met, you ignited a spark within me that I never knew existed. You've shown me what it means to believe in the power of trust, to embrace the vulnerability that comes with love. You've stood by my side through challenges and triumphs, and I promise to do the same for you. With you, I've found a partner, a confidant, and a love that knows no bounds. Today, I vow to cherish and support you in all that you do, to be your rock and your safe haven. I promise to build a life filled with laughter, adventure, and unwavering love. I am forever grateful for you, and I can't wait to embark on this beautiful journey as your wife."

Ethan's gaze never wavered from Isabella's. His voice carried the depth of his feelings. "Isabella, you've brought light into my life in ways I never thought possible. Your strength, your dedication, and your belief in justice have inspired me. You've shown me the power of resilience and the beauty of vulnerability. With you, I've found a love that is both my anchor and my wings. Today, I promise to stand by your side through every storm, to lift you up when you need it, and to hold you close in times of joy. I vow to be your partner in every sense of the word, to support your dreams, and nurture our shared aspirations. As we walk this path together, I am excited to create a life filled with love and endless possibilities. I am honored to call you my wife, and I can't wait to see where our journey takes us."

The exchange of vows was a poignant moment. Their words were a testament to the challenges they had overcome and the love that had blossomed between them. Tears glistened in the eyes of their loved ones, who had seen their journey firsthand. Following the ceremony, the reception unfolded under a starlit sky. The venue transformed into a wonderland of light. The twinkling fairy lights and lanterns cast a magical ambiance. Guests dined on gourmet cuisine and raised a toast to the newlyweds, their glasses clinking in celebration.

***

They danced together under the starlit sky during their wedding reception. Isabella's head rested against Ethan's shoulder, and he held her close. Their hearts were beating as one. In the midst of the celebration, they shared a quiet moment of reflection. They honored the memories of their parents. Isabella's eyes glistened with unshed tears as she thought of her parents. Her father's gentle guidance and her mother's support were memories that filled her. She yearned for their presence as she took this momentous step in her life. They had been her pillars of strength. She wished they could be there to witness the culmination of her journey. Their absence left an ache, but their love remained a guiding light.

"We're building something beautiful together, aren't we?" Isabella whispered, her voice tinged with both sadness and hope.

Ethan tightened his embrace and nodded, his gaze fixed on the stars above. "Yes, we are. And I believe our parents are watching over us, guiding us every step of the way."

Isabella smiled through her tears, finding solace in his words. "I like to think that they're here with us in spirit, celebrating this day and showering us with their love."

"Absolutely," Ethan agreed, his voice filled with conviction. "They may not be present, but their legacy lives on through us, in the love we share and the journey we've embarked upon."

The couple's first dance was a choreographed blend of elegance and passion that left their guests in awe. As they twirled across the dance floor, their connection was palpable – a bond strengthened by trials and fortified by love.

Throughout the evening, laughter and joy filled the air as guests enjoyed live music, heartfelt speeches, and the warmth of each other's company. Even the wedding cake, a masterpiece of artistry, was cut with shared laughter. The dance floor remained alive with celebratory energy.

As they swayed to the music, their hearts beat in sync. It was a reminder that the love of their parents continued to shape their lives, infusing their union with a sense of purpose and resilience. At that moment, as they held each other close, Isabella and Ethan felt an unbreakable connection.

*** THE END***

ABOUT THE AUTHOR

Kathy Winslower is a gifted storyteller with a passion for weaving tales of love, resilience, and triumph. With her captivating narratives and richly drawn characters, she takes readers on unforgettable journeys that explore the depths of human emotions and the power of love to transform lives.

Born with an insatiable curiosity and a love for words, Kathy began her writing journey at a young age, filling countless notebooks with her imaginative stories. As she grew older, her passion for storytelling only deepened, leading her to pursue a career as a novelist.

Drawing inspiration from her own experiences and the world around her, Kathy's writing is characterized by its heartfelt authenticity and emotional depth. She skillfully delves into the complexities of relationships, capturing the raw and tender moments that shape her characters' lives.

When she's not immersed in her writing, Kathy can be found exploring nature, seeking inspiration from the beauty of the world around her. She believes that every moment holds the potential for a story, and it is her mission to capture those moments and share them with her readers.